To A who has the patience of a saint, the wisdom of a sage, and the humor of a stand-up comedian trapped in a sitcom.

Ice, Love, & Other Penalties

USA TODAY BESTSELLING AUTHOR
CLAUDIA BURGOA

Also By Claudia Burgoa

Be sure to sign up for my newsletter where you'll receive news about upcoming releases, sneak previous, and also FREE books from other bestselling authors.

Ice, Love, & Other Penalties is also available in Audio

The Baker's Creek Billionaire Brothers Series

Loved You Once

A Moment Like You

Defying Our Forever

Call You Mine

As We Are

Yours to Keep

Collide with Me

Paradise Bay Billionaire Brothers

My Favorite Night

Faking The Game

Can't Help Love

Along Came You

My Favorite Mistake

The Way of Us

Meant For Me

Finally Found You

Where We Belong

Heartwood Lake Secret Billionaires

A Place Like You

Dirty Secret Love

Love Unlike Ours

Through It All

Better than Revenge

Fade into us

An Unlikely Story

Hard to love

Against All Odds Series

Wrong Text, Right Love

Didn't Expect You

Love Like Her

Until Next Time, Love

Something Like Love

Accidentally in Love

Decker Family Novels

Unexpected Everlasting:

Suddenly Broken

Suddenly Us

Somehow Everlasting:
Almost Strangers
Strangers in Love

Perfect Everlasting:
Who We Are
Who We Love

Us After You

Covert Affair Duet:
After The Vows
Love After Us

The Downfall of Us:
The End of Me
When Forever Finds Us

Requiem for Love:
Reminders of Her
The Symphony of Us

Impossibly Possible:
The Lies About Forever
The Truth About Love

Ice, Love, & Other Penalties

Second Chance Sinners :
Pieces of Us
Somehow Finding Us

The Spearman Brothers

Maybe Later
Then He Happened
Once Upon a Holiday
Almost Perfect

Luna Harbor

Finally You
Perfectly You
Always You
Truly You

My One
My One Regret
My One Desire

The Everhart Brothers

Fall for Me
Fight for Me

Perfect for Me

Forever with Me

Kentbury Tales

Christmas in Kentbury

Fall in Kentbury

Standalones

Chasing Fireflies

Until I Fall

Finding My Reason

Something Like Hate

Someday, Somehow

Chaotic Love Duet

Begin with You

Back to You

Co-writing

Holiday with You

Home with You

Here with You

All my books are interconnected standalone, except for the duets, but if you want a reading order, I have it here ↪
Reading Order

"To love at all is to be vulnerable. Love anything and your heart will be wrung and possibly broken." — C.S. Lewis, "The Four Loves"

Prologue

Indie

Love is, for some, the ultimate dream. For me, it's a waste of time.

Romance is nothing but heartache as far as I could see.

Don't believe me? My biological mother couldn't live with herself after my biological father died in a car accident. The doctors were able to save me through an emergency C-section. She hadn't been able to bear the grief and loss of my father. I may have survived, but she did not.

I was a lucky girl, though. Jacob and Pria Decker offered to foster me from the moment I took my first breath.

They were in the NICU for the first three weeks, then took me home, hoping one day they would be able to adopt me. There's a happy beginning to that story. Soon, I became Indigo Faye Decker—Indie for short.

Mom and Dad have shown me all about family and love. They love me just the same as they do my siblings, even if I don't share their blood. That kind of love is easy to understand. The romantic one . . . well, in my opinion it sucks.

It's a lie.

It breaks people, and some don't even survive—like my mother. If that's not enough, take one of my oldest brothers, for example. Gabriel lost his first girlfriend at the age of sixteen. He was utterly devastated for a long time. Then came Ameline, and though she brought a smile to his face, it disappeared when she moved across the country to create a new life. That type of love broke him into a million pieces.

Then there's my sister Harper. Her fiancé was physically, emotionally, and mentally abusing her for years. That worthless piece of trash had destroyed a part of my vibrant, confident older sister.

Who wants to be with someone if, at the end of the day, they're going to make you feel useless? Not me.

I wish I could say this was just me being an observer, but I once was in love, and he . . . Well, he destroyed me.

The first time I saw him, he was a whirlwind on ice, a blur of navy blue, gold, and white. His sheer talent made my heart race faster than the skaters on the rink. His name was Frederick, and in the glow of the rink lights, he seemed more myth than man, a hero in a hockey jersey. He was my oldest brother Jude's friend. Freddie was a fixture in our home, but to me, he was untouchable, a dream wrapped in the harsh reality of ice.

It wasn't just his skill that captivated me. It was the

easy laughter, the way his dark brown eyes crinkled at the edges when he smiled, and how he seemed to fill any room he entered with an infectious energy. To everyone else, he was Freddie, the talented hockey player destined for greatness. To me, he was the guy who made my heart do somersaults every time he ruffled my hair and called me "kid." If only I'd known the kind of man who lurked beneath the surface.

But as the years slipped by, the gap between Freddie and me seemed to shrink. I went from being Jude's annoying little sister to someone he actually saw. Our conversations stretched beyond the polite small talk, delving into dreams, fears, and his future. A future I wanted to be a part of. His hopes for the big leagues, knowing the scouts that were already circling. I hung onto every word, secretly dreaming of a future where I was more than just a spectator in his life.

After graduating, he still came around our house to visit us. Though, secretly I always thought it was me who he was looking for. Our friendship grew as I became older. At least, that's what I thought.

And when I started college, we texted often. Then, there was that one day when his team was in New York to play, and he came to my little studio apartment after the game. I felt so lucky.

Lucky that he had finally turned those dark eyes in my direction. Lucky that we were finally crossing the line from friends to more. At first, I thought my luck had finally turned, but I couldn't have been more wrong.

He finally saw me as Indie.

I wasn't Jude's little sister.

I wasn't the girl with the childish crush.

He saw me as me—someone who saw him, not just the hockey player, but the boy who laughed too loud, who loved cheesy horror movies, and who had the power to make my heart race with just a glance.

The innocent eighteen-year-old full of love still remembers that night.

When an unexpected visitor had turned my quiet evening upside down. Someone had knocked on my door. When I opened it, it was him, Frederick. I knew the Boston Blizzards were playing the New York Guardians that night but seeing him on my doorstep . . . something shifted in the atmosphere of my small, art-filled space. There he stood, looking effortlessly charismatic.

"I hope I'm not intruding," he'd said, his voice carrying that familiar warmth, tinged with an edge of something more—excitement, perhaps, or anticipation. "I couldn't be this close and not see you."

His words, simple as they were, struck a chord deep within me. It was as if, in that moment, he truly saw me.

"Hey, Freddie," I said as I finally found my words.

"Finally, I get to do this," he said, his voice deep and commanding as he closed the distance between us. Before I could react, his lips were on mine, demanding and forceful. I froze, unsure of how to respond. This wasn't the gentle, tentative first kiss I had imagined. It was something else entirely.

He pulled back, his eyes searching mine for a response. I couldn't find my voice, so I simply stared at him, my heart still racing. He took this as an invitation, and his lips were on mine again, this time with more urgency.

My mind was reeling. This was wrong, wasn't it?

But at the same time, it felt so right. His hands roamed my body, igniting a fire within me that I had never felt before. I couldn't help but respond, my own hands exploring his muscular frame.

I winced as he pushed my panties down, his fingers grazing my skin. I wasn't ready for this, was I? But it was too late to turn back now. He was already unbuttoning his pants, revealing his impressive length. I gasped as he entered me, the pain sharp and intense.

"Stop, please, stop," I whispered, my voice barely audible over the pounding of my heart, but he didn't listen to my plea. Instead, he dove deeper into his own urgency, his movements became more frantic, as if trying to escape from something within himself rather than connecting with me.

That night marked the end of my love story, the kind of ending that doesn't make it into the fairy tales. It was the night he finally kissed me, the night I thought would seal our love, but instead, it unraveled the very fabric of my being. It was as if he took everything from me, leaving me hollow.

I chastised myself, laughter bitter and hollow resonating in my mind. How could I have been so naïve? To believe that he could ever love me was foolish. He proved as much when, after he was done, he walked away without a backward glance. The one time I dared to reach out to him, he coldly told me to leave him alone. Claimed he was too busy for a "child" like me. He even threatened me with a restraining order if I dared to contact him again.

Love, I've come to realize, is a fool's game. It tempts you with promises of forever, only to leave you shattered in its wake.

Haunted by the fear of ending up like my biological mother—to unlife myself after the loss of the man she loved—a cascade of nightmares began to plague me. Night after night, they serve as a cruel reminder of my stupidity, transforming my life.

Despite the mayhem that boils within me, I strive to live a semblance of a normal life. Yet, when the night falls and the world quiets, the fear of closing my eyes is palpable. The darkness isn't just the absence of light. It's a canvas for my deepest fears to paint their horrors.

But in the light of day, I wear my mask well. Everyone in my family just thinks that I have debilitating anxiety, which interferes with some aspects of my life. Yet, I still smile, I laugh, and I pretend that I'm okay. Despite the fact that beneath the surface there's a constant battle raging—a battle to find peace with my past, to forgive myself.

Of course, I tread carefully, guarding my heart against the possibility of being shattered once more.

Chapter One

Tyberius

I'M PACING back and forth in my kitchen, the phone pressed so tightly against my ear that my knuckles shine white. Gemma's apologetic voice filters through, each word landing like a blow as she explains why she can't work for us anymore.

"I'm so sorry to do this last minute . . ." Gemma's voice cracks over the phone.

I squeeze my eyes shut, massaging my forehead as the beginnings of a headache throb to life. The sun hasn't even peeked over the horizon yet, but Gemma's news makes it feel like this day is doomed before it's even begun.

"It's just not going to work out . . ." she continues, her words fading to a murmur under the sudden rush of blood pounding in my ears.

My stomach drops, a sense of foreboding washing over me as I brace for what I know is coming next. This can't be happening. This is actually a lot worse than when my girlfriend broke up with me a few years back.

"I can't be a mother," she said, so I showed her the door and that was that.

Did it hurt? It didn't break my heart, but she made me realize that I had spent two years with a shallow woman.

But losing my nanny—well, this is definitely something I can't handle as easily. What the fuck am I going to do now?

". . . I've enjoyed working with Myra—she's a wonderful child," she continues. "But a family emergency has come up unexpectedly, and I need to leave town immediately. And honestly, I won't be able to come back. I understand this puts you in a difficult position, and I truly apologize."

I stop pacing and grip the edge of the granite counter, knuckles whitening. Irritation and panic swell within me, though I try to keep my emotions hidden. There's no denying that I'm upset at her sudden resignation. I should tell her we have a contract. I paid for her relocation, on top of a hefty bonus and . . . what's the point? She'll still leave because her family needs her.

Isn't that what we all do? Family comes first.

"I understand," I reply finally, struggling to keep my voice steady. What's the point of yelling over the phone when it won't fix anything? "Family comes first. I hope everything is okay on your end." I exhale and try to inject warmth into my tone. "We'll miss you around here. Myra loves spending time with you. And if you ever return to Seattle, we'll be happy to have you back."

There's a pause, and I picture Gemma weighing her next words. "Thank you, Mr. Brynes. That means a lot," she says softly. "Myra is a bright, kind girl and I've loved being with her. I've written down some notes and meal plans to help with the transition of whoever you find next. I'll email them to you as soon as I hang up." Another hesitant sigh. "I wish I could give you more notice, but I really do have to leave as soon as possible. I'm so sorry."

The finality in her voice hits me harder than a slap shot to the chest. I'm not just losing a nanny. We're losing the only person who knows how to take care of Myra. And what the fuck am I supposed to do now? Finding someone on such short notice feels as impossible as scoring a game-winning goal in the final seconds of overtime. I've got a game tomorrow, and come next week, I'm supposed to be on a flight to New York.

There's no way I can bring my almost six-year-old along without adult supervision, or that I could magically conjure up a nanny who can stay with her for the next . . . twelve years?

"Thanks for everything," I say tightly, the words barely escaping as I fight back a swell of frustration and panic. I muster up a semblance of politeness before saying, "Safe travels, and I hope everything works out for you."

As I hang up the phone, the weight of my new reality crashes into me like a brutal check into the boards. Panic claws at the edges of my composure. What the fuck am I supposed to do now?

The thought of calling in sick crosses my mind, a laughable solution given the circumstances. *Sorry, coach, but I can't make it because my daughter has no one to look after her.* As the captain of the Seattle Sasquatches, the newest team in the league supposedly built from the best players available. All eyes are on us, waiting to see if we measure up to the hype.

Do we deserve the hype? It doesn't matter if it's true or not. We have a few weeks to prove this team can go all the way and win the Stanley Cup—and the season opener is just a few days away. And with the clock ticking down to the season's start, the absence of even one player—especially the captain—could derail everything we've worked for in the past few months.

Dragging a hand through my hair, I let out a breath that feels like it's been punched out of me. The timing couldn't be worse. I can't just play hooky because my daughter needs adult supervision. Also, I can't just leave Myra unattended.

I try to focus on preparing a pot of coffee, keeping my hands busy in hopes my mind will follow suit and calm the fuck down. But my thoughts keep drifting back to my daughter and how I'm going to manage this season as a nanny-less single dad while also serving as captain of a brand-new NHL team.

There has to be a way to make this work. I've done it since Myra was born—but I found a nanny right

Ice, Love, & Other Penalties

away who helped me. Now . . . I can't even call a family member to come to my aid. Back when we lived in Florida, I could ask my mother. More times than not—and after giving her a hefty amount of money—she would agree to care for her only granddaughter for a couple of hours.

When we moved to Seattle, she said she would stay in Florida. According to her, she's too old to keep up with my daughter. Since when is fifty-three too old? I should remind her of our conversation the next time she decides to travel to some remote location with her friend or some new beau and asks for money.

With no other options, I reluctantly pick up my phone again and scroll to make a few necessary calls. The first is to Jude Decker, general manager and owner of the Seattle Sasquatches. Anxiety twists my stomach into knots as I tap his name, dreading having this conversation but knowing it can't wait.

Jude answers briskly after the second ring, his gravelly voice alert despite the early hour. "Decker speaking."

I clear my throat, steeling my nerves. No way around it now—I have to explain my situation and hope he can offer some miracle solution. But the next words stick briefly in my dry throat as the clock ticks down to my expected arrival at the rink.

"Mr. Decker, Tyberius Brynes here," I begin, my voice catching slightly as I cradle the phone on my shoulder and fill a mug with steaming coffee. "Sorry to call so early, but do you have a few minutes to chat?"

"Please, call me Jude," he corrects warmly. I can hear the smile in his gravelly voice. "No need to be so formal. And for you, captain, I've always got time. What seems to be the trouble?"

I squeeze my eyes shut, picturing my daughter's smiling face to gather courage. Taking a steely breath, I admit, "I'm in a difficult position. My nanny unexpectedly quit this morning due to a family emergency." I sip the cooling coffee, trying not to panic. "As you're aware, it's just my daughter Myra and me. With no friends or family nearby, there's no one to watch her while I'm at the rink." I glance anxiously at the clock as dread twists my insides. "I'm expected on the ice in two hours."

Jude is silent for a moment. I imagine the gears spinning in his head. "Have you contacted the relocation team for help in finding a replacement? They're pretty good at what they do."

I scrub a hand over my jaw, feeling the rough shadow of stubble under my palm. "No. I . . . when we were negotiating my contract and relocating here, my nanny almost quit on me then too. I asked the relocation team for help to secure childcare options, but they said they didn't handle those kinds of services."

"I'll be addressing this issue with relocation directly," Jude states, voice hardened by irritation. "Assisting with urgent family matters should be a priority service they provide. I understand you need to look after your daughter." He sighs heavily. "But, we need you at practice today and on the ice tomorrow night. It's the first preseason game and that's not something you can miss."

I rake a frustrated hand through my hair. "Believe me, I know. I don't want to let the team down, especially not right before the season starts. I'm trying to figure something out, but I might need some flexibility today. Maybe come in late after I get Myra to school and leave early to pick her up. Hopefully by then I can track down a sitter for the game at least."

Jude goes quiet and I picture his face creased in a frown as he contemplates my suggestion. His lengthening silence makes my stomach knot with unease. Is he having second thoughts about having a single dad for his star player before the season has even begun?

"Well, have you gotten to know anyone locally who could help out in a pinch?" he finally asks.

I wince, shoulders slumping. "Honestly? No. Between practices and Myra, I haven't had much time to socialize."

"Okay, let me make a few calls then," Jude states. "Can you get Myra ready and bring her to the training facilities? We'll set up a space for her to hang out while you practice. I'll alert the staff to make sure she's comfortable and looked after. My driver can transport her to and from school."

I exhale in relief, the tight band around my chest loosening slightly. "That would be amazing. Thank you, I really appreciate it, Mr. Deck—Jude," I swiftly correct.

"What about tomorrow night though?" he presses. "You think you'll have childcare arranged for the game?"

My hand rakes through my hair again, frustration mounting. "With everything going on, finding a sitter by then might be unlikely," I admit, failing to keep the uncertainty from my voice.

"You seem unsure. Listen, consider it handled," Jude announces. "Get Myra fed and bring her in with you. I give you my word, she'll have someone utterly trustworthy watching her by puck drop tomorrow night.

I'll make sure the relocation director finds you a suitable nanny, even if I have to drag her here myself to interview candidates in person—or even better, she'll nanny for you."

There's a flare of fierce satisfaction in his tone. Like he's actually looking forward to reaming out the director who screwed me over. I shouldn't take pleasure in the threat, but I'm actually happy that she'll pay for all the shit she's put me through so far.

"Thank you, si—" I catch myself with a wince. "Jude. I appreciate you going to bat for me."

"We take care of our people here," he reminds firmly. "So let me handle logistics while you focus on your game and that little girl. My staff will make sure Myra is well-cared for. You just play your best hockey tomorrow night and leave the rest to me, you hear?"

It seems like such an easy solution, yet the weight on my shoulders doesn't lift. Something might go totally wrong and I'm not ready to retire. Not yet.

Chapter Two

Indigo

"Ugh, shaddup," I mumble, pulling a pillow over my head as my phone's abrasive buzzing shreds the pre-dawn quiet. Who would dare interrupt my slumber? "Whoever's interrupting my beauty rest can leave a message."

I burrow deeper under the covers, squeezing my eyes shut and willing sleep to reclaim me for those last precious pre-dawn hours. But the phone continues buzzing relentlessly atop my nightstand, intent on jangling my already-frayed nerves.

"Meow," David Meowie complains, settling right atop my pillow and head.

Rigby begins nudging my stomach simultaneously, as if the buzzing signals it's clearly time to wake up and feed them.

"One pest at a time," I grumble, extracting David Meowie and placing him gently on the bed. Rigby continues prodding persistently. With an irritated sigh, I flop an arm out, fingers fumbling across the nightstand for the offending device. Caller ID flashes Jude's name—the only one of my meddling brothers who would risk this ungodly intrusion.

"This better be important enough to disturb my sleep," I grit out by way of greeting, not hiding my irritation. Sometimes I swear I feel more like the elder sibling, catering to Jude's endless needs.

Rigby bumps his head insistently under my hand, reminding me food takes priority over venting. "Yes, yes, breakfast is coming," I assure him resignedly, already swinging my legs out of bed and taking a seat on the mattress. David Meowie springs lithely into the warm spot I've vacated, circling to knead the sheets with delicate paws. At least one of us gets to lounge comfortably this morning.

"Rise and shine, princess." Jude's voice comes through, he's annoyingly chipper given the ungodly hour. "Hope I didn't wake you," he adds, not even attempting to sound sincere.

I snort, scrubbing the bleariness from my eyes as I finally leave the bed. Rigby wags his tail, panting impatiently while David Meowie winds figure eights around my legs. "You called just to wake me up," I accuse.

As David Meowie continues to weave around my ankles, Rigby nudges my leg impatiently. I stride toward the kitchen, the pair trailing expectantly. "Okay, okay, breakfast is coming," I assure them, stifling a yawn. I scoop out portions into their bowls before turning to the espresso machine to start my hot water.

"So what's so important it couldn't wait for a decent hour, Jude?" I tweak David Meowie's ear playfully as he passes to eat, eliciting an offended mewl. I straighten, opening the fridge and grabbing a yogurt.

Once I have my mug filled with hot water, and my breakfast set, I meander back toward my room. During all this time my brother hasn't said a word. Not a one.

"This better be good. You're interrupting prime relaxation time," I warn, lowering myself onto the rumpled sheets. Rigby hops up to keep me company, resting his head on my leg as I open my breakfast. "I'm waiting for the life-or-death explanation, big brother."

Jude tsks. "That's no way to greet your favorite brother and general manager."

"Alright Decker, cut the dramatics," I grumble, unable to stifle my irritation. "What's so damn important that you had to call at the ass-crack of dawn and couldn't wait until a reasonable hour?"

"I swear this is really important," he claims.

"Uh-huh. I'm sure it's important." Skepticism drips from my words. "Well, like I've told you before, the answer is no. I have zero interest in coming over to kick out another one of your awkward one-night stands."

My thirty-five-year-old brother is a grown-ass man who needs to get his personal life in order instead of relying on me to tidy up his messes. I'm not here to shame his lifestyle choices, but Jude should take some responsibility and stop creating uncomfortable situations.

"It's simple, Jude—just tell them upfront you don't do relationships and would appreciate it if they leave right after you fuck. No sleepovers," I say bluntly. Crude maybe, but subtlety clearly hasn't worked on him yet. "Set some boundaries before you invite them over. Or get a hotel room and skip the awkward morning-after."

Maybe he should give something real a shot, tell his friend with benefits . . . No, it's best I don't meddle in his love life, or he might start managing mine. I press my lips together firmly. No more kicking out one-night stands for him.

"I wouldn't call my sisters to do my dirty work," he has the audacity to say.

I snort, wholly unconvinced by his denial. "Sure, except our sister Lyric has also had to shoo out a few awkward morning-afters herself recently." I allow an edge of sarcastic exasperation to creep into my tone. "So let's not pretend this is an isolated issue."

Jude sighs heavily through the phone. "Okay fine, fair enough. But that's not why I called . . ."

I roll my eyes but take pity on him. "Fine. What's the current crisis then?" I ask, stifling a yawn and settling more comfortably against the pillows. Rigby plops onto my stomach and I lazily scratch behind his ears, bracing for Jude's latest convoluted excuse or favor.

"Tyberius Brynes," he states, an undercurrent of tension in his usual easygoing tone.

I sit straighter. "Right, number twenty-three and the

team captain." No surprise it involves the Sasquatches—everything in Jude's orbit does.

"Look at you, already an expert on the lineup," Jude says proudly. "This is why our team will be successful. The two owners are not only savvy about hockey, but we both care about our staff and players."

I snort. "It's your team, not mine. Once it's running smoothly, I'm out of here, remember?"

"For now, consider yourself my relocation director," Jude fires back before I can argue. "Brynes's nanny just quit on him. Family emergency or something. He's scrambling, and we need a quick fix."

Despite Jude's typical laid-back nature, the quiet urgency and concern in his tone tells me this problem requires immediate handling. I'm already heading to my closet to pick out an acceptable work outfit, David Meowie twining around my ankles while Rigby watches curiously. I need to shower and prep for whatever ploy Jude has cooked up that involves me somehow.

"Well, you know I don't actually have the title of relocation director, right?" I toss over my shoulder as I rifle through blouses and slacks, selecting a nondescript black ensemble appropriate for damage control.

"Well, apparently you told Brynes we don't handle childcare?" Jude snaps, irritation bleeding into his voice.

I pause while rifling through shoe options, wincing at his irritated tone. Heels or flats? Should I hang up or help him? So many choices . . .

"Listen, I talked to a lot of the guys those first frenzied weeks," I hedge, scrambling to recall specifics. "Handling housing assignments for the influx of new staff and players, conversations blur together . . ." Even as I say it, I know it's no excuse. Jude brought me on to support these players, and I clearly dropped the ball with this Brynes guy.

After a couple of seconds, I do remember my email exchanges with Ty Brynes. We'd been overwhelmed with all the people who moved to Seattle. Though, I did put a system in place that made it a little less daunting. Except, there's one player who refused to fill out any specifics and just wanted lists to choose from.

A list of schools, doctors . . . I could've gotten a list if he had given me any info.

Then there was the house—again, he chose not to give me a must-haves list for that too and, well, he lives in a big ass mansion outside of Seattle. His fault, not mine.

"This guy is a diva," I tell Jude once I remember exactly why I wasn't very helpful, according to him. "You say he's good, but in my book he's not the kind of person who deserves to be on this team."

"Regardless, since I'm busy with training, it falls to you now to handle this," Jude states, an undercurrent of frustration entering his typically mellow tone. I picture him nearly crushing his phone, staunchly defending his star player.

Even though I'd love to claim this isn't my responsibility, duty holds my tongue. I rub my temples, striving to view this objectively despite spiraling guilt. "Okay, wait. What exactly do you need me to do here?"

"We have several options. You can call around and get us a nanny for his daughter Myra or . . ." Jude trails off leadingly.

I whip around from the closet, startling David Meowie who was snoozing atop a pile of rejected blouses. "Oh, no. No. No way. You did *not* just nominate me to play super-aunt-nanny until I find a replacement?" I cry incredulously into the receiver.

"Bingo. You're the best person for the job, Indie-bear. You know it," he says, a hint of pleading in his voice. "It's just until *you* find a suitable, trustworthy replacement. We can't just leave the kid with some unknown person that walks through the door."

I fling another hanger back onto the rack, disgruntled. Rigby lifts his head, watching placidly from his dog bed as I storm past. So much for a professional look—babysitting calls for comfy clothes instead.

"Sure, make Indigo the team's Mary Poppins because I'm obviously unoccupied," I shoot back, rolling my eyes.

"It's not babysitting. It's . . . strategic team support," Jude counters, barely containing a laugh.

I can't help but roll my eyes, even though he can't see me. "Strategic team support. Right." I retort, hands on hips. "And what makes you think I'm the woman for the job? My outstanding nurturing skills or my vast experience with children?"

"You're organized, you're great with people, and you've been handling the team's relocation like a pro. Plus, all our nieces and nephews love you," he argues, ticking off each point as if it's the most logical conclusion in the world.

The tension in my back ratchets up another notch. Rigby pads over, resting his chin on my leg comfortingly. I scratch behind his ears, to release some of the tension building on my back. "I'm happy to help find a nanny, but babysitting is not in my job description," I reply pointedly.

"Indie, we need our captain for the opening game,"

Jude insists. "Do you really think we'll find better care by then?"

I refuse to reply, knowing Jude will likely strongarm me into becoming the team's permanent babysitter. I should've gone back to school like Dad said rather than getting roped into Jude's schemes.

"Come on, Indie-bear. I need my baby sister to come through. Please, just one more time."

Why me? I almost say out loud. I swear, he's wearing me out. It's impossible to say no to Jude, especially when I can hear the genuine need in his voice. He's been working on having a hockey team in Seattle for years. I'm the only one he confided in and told about it.

Not even Gabe, his twin, heard of it until this was a done deal. He was afraid that everyone in the family would think it was just another venture he'd abandon by the end of the month.

I know how much it means to him, and I want him to succeed more than anyone.

As little desire as I have to play surrogate parent, family supports each other unconditionally. With a resigned sigh, I meet Rigby's sympathetic brown eyes. Even David Meowie gives a plaintive meow from my pile of clothes, as if reminding me of my duty.

"Fine, I'll help *temporarily* care for the kid," I concede grudgingly. "Strictly short-term, until an exceptionally vetted nanny is in charge."

"Temporary. Got it." Jude exhales, relief evident even over the phone. "You're a lifesaver, Indie-bear. Ty and the team owe you one."

"They owe me more than one. I'm adding this to my ever-growing tab. And Jude? Next time you decide

Ice, Love, & Other Penalties

to volunteer me for something, at least have the decency to ask me after I've had my coffee."

His laughter fills the line, warm and familiar. "Deal. Thanks, Sis. You're the best."

"Yeah, yeah," I reply, Jude's laughter dissolving the last of my irritation. A smile tugs at my lips as David Meowie bumps his fuzzy head against my leg insistently. I reach down to give him a good chin scratch, eliciting a rumbling purr.

"Send all of Tyberius's info my way since I won't be going into headquarters now," I continue, meandering toward the kitchen. Rigby trots over to stand hopefully by his empty food bowl. "Forward his daughter's schedule too if you have it."

"Will do. I'll text contact details and email additional paperwork," Jude confirms.

As we hang up, I'm already mentally rearranging my day, slotting in a trip to Ty's place and a crash course in Myra 101. This isn't how I planned to spend my day, but family—in all its forms—comes first.

I brew an extra bold cappuccino, loading it with mounds of whipped cream and drizzling it liberally with chocolate sauce—something tells me I'll need the fortification. Cradling the sugar concoction, I shuffle back to my room to change.

"Well, boys, looks like we've got an interesting day ahead," I announce to my furry companions. Rigby gives an enthusiastic tail wag which I optimistically interpret as wholehearted support. "Since we're not going to the office, I'll take you to grandma's house or see who can be with you today."

Maybe this spontaneous adventure will be worthwhile solely thanks to the IOU it earns me from Jude.

Chapter Three

Tyberius

Hoping that Jude Decker wasn't just overpromising so he would get me to the rink on time, I finish my coffee with a sigh and then head upstairs to wake Myra up.

I open the door to her room slowly, wincing as it creaks, and tiptoe across the plush carpet on quiet feet. Early morning light filters softly through the curtains, casting a peaceful glow about the room. Myra is curled among a sea of blankets and a mountain of stuffed animals, her chest gently rising and falling in sleep's embrace.

"Good morning, sunshine," I whisper, brushing a featherlight kiss to her head.

Slowly, she drifts back from the land of dreams, her long lashes fluttering as her green eyes blink open to meet mine.

"Morning, Daddy," she mumbles, her voice a sweet, drowsy melody that fills the room with warmth. A big yawn stretches across her face and she reaches for the sky, fingers unfurling like a cat waking to sunlight.

"How did you sleep, pumpkin?" I ask, perching on the edge of her bed, unable to hold back a smile as she rubs the last remnants of sleep from her eyes.

"Good . . . I dreamt we had a real cat, and you promised to buy me a unicorn," she whispers, her face lighting up with the remembered magic of her dreams.

I poke her nose playfully. "That sounds wonderful, but I don't think it's something we can do right now," I say ruefully.

"I know, unicorns are tricky to find in this world." She grins, showcasing the gap where her front tooth used to be. "But you can always bring a kitty home."

With what I'm about to tell her, a unicorn would be a great consolation prize. I mean, this poor child has gone through too many changes since . . . Well, since she was born.

First, her mother decided she wasn't fit to raise a kid. After that, we moved around twice. There were also all the trips she took with me to games because I didn't want her to stay at home with the nanny for days. This was the first year she would have stayed with Gemma while I traveled to games.

Maybe signing here wasn't the wisest choice at my age. As a free agent I can pick my team, but some franchises get leery of players nearing retirement who risk more injuries. Still, it wasn't like I could refuse the generous offer. Providing for Myra has to be my priority, even if it means major life shifts.

"But cats are pretty and my teacher said they're self-rentable." Myra pipes up hopefully, her green eyes round and pleading. "My teacher said so."

I chuckle, poking her nose again. "I think you mean self-reliant, munchkin."

She scrunches her nose. "Maybe?"

I can't help but smile. This kid always tries to logic her way into getting what she wants, whether it's cats, unicorns, or . . . Well, the list keeps growing. It's so hard to deny those big puppy-dog eyes.

Before she campaigns for a pony next, I have to break the news. "So Gemma called this morning," I begin gently.

Myra stills, excitement dimming. "Is she gonna be late today? You get to take me to school today?"

"I wish that were the case, sweet pea." I brush a wayward strand of hair from her face, bracing myself. "Actually, she called to let us know she's moving back to Florida. Her family needs her there."

Myra goes very still, processing this shift in her small world. "So, she's not gonna be here today?" she finally asks, voice wobbling with uncertainty.

I draw her into my lap, embracing her close, wishing I could erase the scrunched look from her dear face. "No, baby. What I meant is she won't be coming

Ice, Love, & Other Penalties

back at all. She had to move back to Florida for good," I explain gently, giving her little hand a reassuring squeeze.

Her lip wobbles as she thinks hard. "Can we go to Florida too? I need my family too," she requests plaintively. My heart clenches at her pinched little face. "Grandma could take care of me."

I smooth back her hair, wishing I could grant her request. "I'm sorry, pumpkin, that's just not possible right now. But, hey, today you get to come with me to the ice rink until it's time for school. We'll have a blast together," I say brightly, trying to inject some enthusiasm despite the guilt swirling in my gut.

She gazes at me for a long moment before finally asking in a small voice, "Can I bring Mr. Whiskers?"

"Mr. Whiskers is always welcome," I assure, relieved to see excitement rekindling behind the sheen of tears. Crisis seemingly averted, at least for now. If only I could get a sitter.

"And I don't hafta wear the itchy sweater?" She scrunches her nose worriedly.

"No itchy sweaters today, I promise." I squeeze her hand, then set her back into the bed. "You can pick out your favorite outfit while I get ready. Maybe those leggings with the rainbows you love?"

"Okay, Daddy," she chirps, a spark of excitement finally glimmering in her eyes. "But I get to pick my own breakfast because Gemma's not here, right?"

I laugh softly. "Within reason, baby girl."

Myra slides off the bed to rifle through her clothes, seeming to accept our new reality even if it's not her first choice. I take a deep breath and head to my room to finish getting ready for this unexpected day, hoping I can be half as adaptable as my daughter. That's when the doorbell rings, a simple chime that feels like the starting buzzer of a hockey game I'm unprepared for.

I shuffle down the stairs, raking a hand through my hair, trying futilely to brush off the lingering stress. When I swing open the door, I'm definitely not ready for the woman standing on my doorstep.

Chapter Four

Tyberius

THE WOMAN STANDING before me seems to materialize from a daydream. She's a goddess gracing my doorstep. My mouth goes dry, my words lost in the wake of her arrival, as I stand there, utterly blindsided by her beauty.

She steals my breath away. Heart-shaped face with radiant, flawless olive skin that begs to be touched, lush mouth curved knowingly, sleek hair tumbling over one shoulder . . . I can barely tear my gaze away. Her dark eyes lock with mine, holding a gaze that's both deliberate and teasing. It's as if she's fully aware of the chaos her presence instigates, finding amusement in my uncharacteristic fumbling.

I find myself ensnared, unable to divert my gaze, each detail of her appearance imprinted in my memory with undeniable clarity.

Stop gawking, Brynes. She's probably some lost college girl or . . . Who is she? It doesn't matter. She's too young for you. Don't be a fucking creep, just get rid of her. You have things to do.

Finally, I clear my throat, managing a greeting, "Umm, can I help you?" Mentally kicking myself for sounding like a tongue-tied teenager.

Full lips quirk into a knowing smile and my pulse trips. "It's not how you can help me, but what I can do for you. I'm Indigo Walker." Her voice holds a throaty confidence with an undertone of sass that sets me instantly on edge. "Jude sent me. It sounds like you could use my expertise."

Indigo Walker. The name clicks, along with the realization that this is the person who's been coordinating the team's relocation. I've heard her name in numerous conversations. We were on the phone a few times and I've received her emails, but we've never met in person. Until now.

I look over my shoulder scanning my big ass house. This is the woman who screwed me over.

"And what exactly did Jude send you for?" I ask sharply, crossing my arms over my chest, trying to regain some control. "He said you'd be finding me a nanny right away. So why are you here?"

"He said that, huh?" Her full, well-groomed eyebrow arches in amusement. "Well, I'm here to be your knight in shining armor, obviously."

I scoff, the irritation bubbling up. "Not sure if I can trust you with this."

She tosses her dark hair, eyes flashing. "I'm your only hope, Tyberius Nolan Brynes. You can't afford to push me away."

My scowl deepens at the use of my full name. "You're the reason I'm in this mess. Finding a house was a nightmare." I gesture at the expansive space. "This place could fit ten people when there's only two of us."

She has the audacity to laugh, full and throaty. It's so fucking hard not to find her sexy and not wanting to push her against the wall and punish her with a kiss. Teach her . . . Whoa, this isn't where I should direct my thoughts. What is happening to me?

Sure, she's beautiful but also too young and a stranger who supposedly will be helping me with my current dilemma.

Keep your hands and mouth to yourself, Brynes.

"Firstly, I'm excellent at my job, thank you very much. The housing debacle was a miscommunication." She ticks the points off on her fingers. "You didn't mention needing less space until after you moved into the house. Not my responsibility after the fact."

I open my mouth to argue, but she barrels on, stepping closer. Her sassy smile widens. "Your daughter is almost six. That's school-age, and we have other arrangements for kids her age. However, you never filled out the questionnaire I sent, hence why it was so hard to help you the way I did your other teammates.

Obviously, I wasn't aware that there wasn't a mother. And as for the nanny emergency, consider me your temporary solution. Jude thinks I can handle it, and I agree."

She brushes past me in a whiff of jasmine and sandalwood, breezing through the front door uninvited. "So, Tyberius, let me work my magic while you go back to sulking."

Tossing a coy smile over her shoulder, she makes her way down the hall with the comfortable familiarity of someone who owns the place. I remain rooted in bewildered silence, pulse kicking against my will.

"You coming?" She has the audacity to ask.

I blink, momentarily speechless as she makes herself at home. Clearly, Indigo Walker is a force of nature—direct yet playful. I stride after her, sternly ignoring the charm she exudes so effortlessly. We have more important matters to address. I can handle keeping things strictly professional.

"Sulking is part of the job when you're a single dad and your nanny quits," I retort, regaining some equilibrium.

Indigo laughs again, the vibrant sound filling the foyer. "Well, consider your sulking days over. I'm here now and ready to handle things." She pauses, glancing around inquisitively. "So where's Myra? Time is precious, Brynes."

"Upstairs, probably turning her room into an art studio or rogue science lab by now," I reply, the tension easing from my shoulders. Because maybe, just maybe, the day won't be a disaster after all.

Indigo nods decisively, a plan clearly brewing behind those intelligent eyes. "Perfect. We'll tidy up, fuel up on pancakes, then get her to school. Maybe when I pick her up, we'll have some ice cream because I was raised by a woman who says that since it has milk, it's good for you."

I can't help but chuckle because she's definitely going to get along with Myra. "I have a feeling you two will get along dangerously well."

Indigo's eyes glint. "Well, then, time for introductions."

Chapter Five

Tyberius

As I lead Indigo upstairs to introduce her to Myra, I can't shake the odd feeling that Jude might have just saved more than my day. He may have brought an unstoppable force named Indigo Walker crashing into our lives, and suddenly, the future seems less daunting.

We reach Myra's door and I brace myself, unsure of

what to expect. I push the door open wider, and unsurprisingly there it is, the aftermath of Myra's attempt to dress herself. Nearly her entire wardrobe lies scattered across the carpet.

This is one of the things Gemma did for us. She would pick out her clothes first thing in the morning before breakfast. We had no debates and no second guesses. Now . . . she might spend the entire day just trying to decide if it's a dress or a leggings kind of day.

Myra looks up, her gaze shifting from me to Indigo, and for a moment, there's a silence filled with appraisal.

"Hi, I'm Myra Brynes. Who are you?" Myra's voice cuts through the room, her tone as if she's interviewing a new candidate for a very important position in her almost six-year-old life.

"This is Indigo," I start, glancing at Indigo, hoping she picks up on the cue. "She's going to hang out with you while we find you a new nanny."

Indigo steps forward, a smile playing on her lips. "Hey, there, Myra. I'm Indie. I'm here to make sure we have a fun day together. How does that sound?"

Myra scrutinizes Indigo for a moment longer. "Do you like My Little Ponies?" she finally asks. "They're my favorite, except for baby unicorns. Those are the bestesests."

"The best," I correct her while Indigo pretends to debate her answer.

"I used to watch the show while growing up, but I've lost track of the new ones," she admits. "Baby unicorns are super cute just like Pegasi. My personal favorites are axolotls."

Myra gives her a sharp nod and smiles then asks,

"Can you help me pick what to wear? I can't decide if I want to dress for the ice rink . . . or maybe we can just skip all that and go to Grandma's house in Florida."

Indigo laughs easily, picking her way through the tornado of clothes. "Well, Florida sounds fun, but how about we just focus on school today?" she suggests diplomatically. "I happen to be great at outfit picking. Sometimes I even design dresses with my sister—she's a fashion designer."

Myra's eyes light up. "Can she make me a dress for my birthday?" she requests, then glances at me. "That could be my present, and then we'll move back to Florida, Daddy."

Indigo glances at me, as if looking for a clue about Florida. I shrug because she just came up with that earlier today.

"I'm pretty sure Lyric, my sister, can help us with your birthday dress," Indie states. "Why don't we focus on today, though?" Indigo replies, winking at Myra.

They dive back into the piles of clothing, and I watch amazed as Indigo expertly engages Myra, navigating her strong will rather than dictating. Before long, they've compromised on the perfect outfit—a sparkly purple tulle skirt paired with Myra's favorite hockey jersey, rainbow leggings peeking out the bottom. Mismatched unicorn socks climb her calves.

And for the first time since the nanny quit, I feel a flicker of hope that maybe, just maybe, things will be okay.

"All set," Indigo announces, standing with a grin. Myra twirls happily, giggling as her skirt spins out.

Indigo winks at me over Myra's head. "Now, who wants my world-famous celebration pancakes?"

"World famous, huh?" I raise an eyebrow. "I'll be the judge of that."

As we head to the kitchen, I can't take my eyes off Indigo—the confident sway of her hips, the sleek dark cascade of hair spilling down her back. She moves with innate grace, and I feel an unwanted spark of attraction.

Indigo takes charge of the kitchen, her movements confident and graceful, with Myra eagerly following. I lean against the doorway, arms folded, watching them interact and making sure this arrangement will work—even when it might only last a few days.

The kitchen transforms under Indigo's touch into an almost magical place. Ingredients appear on the countertop as if by magic—flour, eggs, milk, a bottle of maple syrup—all neatly arranged.

"May I crack the eggs?" Myra's voice is hopeful, her eyes wide with anticipation. It's a simple task, yet the fact that she's requesting and not just demanding is a huge change from her usual behavior.

"Of course," Indigo responds, handing over an egg with a gentle smile. "Just tap it on the edge of this bowl."

Holding my breath, I watch as Myra carefully taps the egg, her little face scrunched in concentration. When it cracks successfully into the bowl, she lights up with a brilliant grin.

"Great job, Myra," Indigo exclaims, holding up her hand. Myra enthusiastically high-fives her, bursting with pride at this accomplishment. "Cracking eggs can be tricky, but you nailed it. We'll make an expert chef of you in no time."

Myra beams under the effusive praise, and my heart swells at her unbridled joy.

Under Indigo's patient guidance, Myra carefully measures flour and adds a dash of cinnamon, face adorably concentrated with her effort. Their interaction flows seamlessly and naturally—Indigo's instructions clear yet gentle, Myra following each step precisely with obvious pride.

Soon, the aroma of cooking pancakes fills the warm kitchen, sweet and celebratory, drawing me fully into this domestic scene playing out before me. Indigo dexterously flips a pancake as Myra applauds enthusiastically, her utter delight infectious.

"These are going to be delicious." Indigo winks down at her tiny sous-chef. "All thanks to your help." Myra glows under the praise, then insists on getting the syrup from the counter herself while Indigo transfers the last golden-brown pancake to the serving plate.

"Think we're ready to sample these world-famous pancakes?" Indigo asks playfully, glancing my way.

"If they taste the way they smell, I'm sure they're probably the best in the world," I admit.

Indigo grabs the plate as Myra holds the syrup while leading our procession to the kitchen island where the other two plates are set. At the first bite, I'm struck by their perfection—fluffy, lightly sweet, utterly delicious.

"World-famous could actually be selling them short," I admit, earning a satisfied smile from Indigo and laughter from Myra.

"I think I like you," Myra looks at Indigo.

"The feeling is mutual," Indigo responds. "Glad we'll be able to hang out for a few days."

But what will happen in a few days? What if I can't

find anyone to look after Myra and she has to go and take care of the rest of the team?

I try not to panic, but the tension is back, and how am I supposed to play tomorrow when my life is a clusterfuck again.

Chapter Six

Indigo

"I'm pretty sure Jude hates me," I mutter under my breath, my shoulders slumping.

Why else would he have sent me here, to the wolf's den that is Tyberius Nolan Brynes' home? I'm no Little Red Riding Hood, but while we were having pancakes, I couldn't help feeling like Tyberius might try to eat me for breakfast. Just push me over the counter, pull my

Ice, Love, & Other Penalties

jeans down and run his tongue along my pussy before devouring me with his big mouth.

The thought of him doing that makes my entire body quiver. I wouldn't mind letting him use his tongue on me as long as I can ride his cock a few times.

Damn it, Indie, stop that. His child is right here and your number one rule is not to get tangled up with older guys, even more so if they are hockey players.

No, my number one rule when it comes to men: keep things strictly on my terms, use them once, no emotions involved. If there's something I learned from Frederick is to use them and never let anyone in.

This isn't good.

Not good at all.

"Thank you for doing this," Tyberius says, his voice deep and rough, pulling me back from the edge of my spiraling thoughts.

I muster a casual smile, masking the mayhem inside. "Of course, Tyberius, it's the least we could do for the captain of the team," I reply, striving for a tone of nonchalance.

"Call me Ty," he says, waving his phone. "Text if you need anything. I wish I could tell you where the emergency numbers are, but you know this area better than me."

I smile at him, he seems flustered, nervous or . . . who knows. "She'll be fine, Ty," I assure him.

"Be good to Indigo, pumpkin," he instructs, his hand gently tousling her hair tenderly.

Myra nods vigorously, bouncing on her tiptoes. "I will, Daddy." She then turns and scampers up the stairs as he strides toward the garage, the door clicking shut behind him.

Their departure leaves me alone with the big, bad wolf himself—or at least, the memory of him that I can't seem to shake. Tyberius Nolan Brynes. Even his name seems darkly thrilling as it rolls off my tongue. He had stood over me—all six-foot-three of solid muscle. I'm a tiny five-foot-two in comparison. He could easily pick me up and toss me over his shoulder . . . maybe push me against the wall and . . . I mentally chastise myself, trying to control these vivid daydreams.

But it's almost impossible not to want him. There's something about the rugged, masculine outline of his figure that commands attention—the well-defined jawline, those prominent cheekbones, and a nose that's straight and perfectly proportioned beneath a strong brow.

His hair, tousled yet styled with effortless care, carries streaks of light brown softened by sun-kissed blond highlights. It makes me want to run a hand through his hair. The short, full beard and mustache framing his lips add to his carefree, yet deliberately rugged appearance.

The thought of feeling the rough texture of his beard against my skin when he goes down on me sends a delicious shiver down my spine.

Fuck, what is wrong with me?

Nothing, mind you, I wouldn't mind the razor burn, especially if he makes me come hard.

What I wouldn't give to see him naked?

"Focus," I scold myself, the stern inner voice attempting to break the spell.

This is exactly why you shouldn't have agreed to take this job when Jude offered it—by which I mean being his right-hand woman while he started the team. I shouldn't be around hockey players. They're obviously my kryptonite. The last time I let one in, he broke me. Now . . . I can't afford to be close to Tyberius, who seems to be my type.

Tall, mysterious, and dangerous.

Yep. Tyberius Brynes is most definitely dangerous in far too many ways. I need to find a new nanny now and get as far away from him as possible.

Before I do something very stupid, like fall for him because he seems like a good father or . . . I find myself biting my lip, anxiety beginning to spiral within me.

My heart races uncontrollably, heralding the onset of panic. Breathing becomes difficult, each breath more strained than the last. My hands start to shake, and reality seems to slip away from me. Tyberius shouldn't have this effect on me, his complex life and burdens shouldn't make my heart race this way.

Just when the panic threatens to overwhelm me, a gentle voice pierces through the haze. "Umm, Indie?" It's Myra. "Over here."

Right, I take a deep breath, reminding myself that I have a responsibility. My attraction for her father and everything that it entails doesn't matter. What happened in the past was after all my fault and if this time I'm careful enough nothing will happen to me. Nothing.

"Why don't you come upstairs? We didn't pick out my shoes for today yet," she prompts me.

I snap back to reality, meeting her wide green eyes that remind me so much of her father's. Shoes. Right, we forgot about that.

"Of course, sweetie," I say, plastering a smile on my face when I find her in front of me.

How did I miss this? I need to be more careful with

my thoughts and what I'm doing around her. I can't lose my shit in front of her. I simply can't.

"Let's go find you some fabulous shoes, and after that . . ." I tap my chin, racking my brain for how I'll possibly occupy Myra for the next hour while I try to calm down.

"We can watch TV or play video games after. Gemma and I always do that before school," Myra says brightly, though I suspect she's not being entirely honest.

I also wonder who this Gemma is—her dad's girlfriend? The nanny? I really should have gotten a crash course on Myra before Tyberius rushed out the door.

"Well, since you and I are still getting to know each other, I think it's best if we spend some time bonding," I suggest, gesturing toward the kitchen. "Plus, we should wash the dishes and tidy up your room before I drive you to school."

Myra's face falls into a pout. "But that's not how Gemma does things with me."

I give her a patient smile. "I understand, sweetie. Usually, my niece Cora would be asking me to braid her hair before school. I certainly don't expect you to request the same. I know you two are very different people."

"Yeah, we're not the same at all," Myra says in agreement.

"Exactly." I give her an encouraging nod. "So, it's best if you and I get to know each other and come up with a routine that works for us."

She lets out a resigned sigh, her shoulders slumping. "Okay, but I probably won't like any of this," she grumbles. "We should go back to Florida with my friends."

Ice, Love, & Other Penalties

I bite back a laugh at her dramatics, but then stop and realize that the nanny quitting has just unraveled her feelings about the move.

Maybe this is something we should look into more closely. When I drop her at school, I plan on reminding her teacher that she's not only new to the school but also to the city.

Right now, it's my job to ensure that she feels welcomed. Maybe I can try to set up a few dates with Cora who's around her age. This won't be easy, but I'll make it work.

"Come on, I'm pretty sure we can make this fun," I cajole as we head to the kitchen, Myra dragging her feet on the stairs behind me.

We stand side by side at the sink, where I show Myra how to rinse the dishes before carefully handing them to her to put in the dishwasher. She seems unsure at first, but eventually gets the hang of where things go. As we work, we chat about everything under the sun—her favorite animals (she wants a cat and maybe a dog someday), what she's learning in school, and her friends.

Lucky for her, I come equipped with a cat and a dog who'll be great at helping me with Myra's transition.

After the kitchen is tidy again, we move on to her room. Together, we pick up scattered toys, organize books, and smooth out the crumpled sheets to make her bed. It's not just about getting the cleaning done but also spending quality time together and teaching her responsibility. By the time we finish, the room looks like a brand-new space, and the pride shining in Myra's eyes makes every bit of effort worthwhile.

We even pick up a pair of shoes that match her

outfit—and I convince her to switch her mismatched socks too.

"All ready for school?" I ask.

She self-consciously touches her hair and the messy ponytail she didn't want me to touch earlier, a hint of uncertainty in her bright green eyes. "Would you mind making it pretty?"

"Of course, sweetie." I pick up a brush from her dresser and gently work through the tangles, then sweep her wavy hair up into a cute, updo, adding a bow I find in a drawer.

With her hair done, it's time to get in the car. The drive to school is brief, and even though the streets are bustling with the morning rush and the school parking lot is teeming with cars, luck is on our side. I find the perfect parking spot at Dad's recording company, conveniently located across the street from Myra's school. Spotting his car already there, I make a mental note to drop by for a visit.

Hand in hand, we make our way into the school, navigating through the lively corridors to her kindergarten classroom. Letting go of her hand at the door feels unexpectedly hard, a pang of separation anxiety pulling at my heartstrings. Yet, she dashes into the colorful, inviting room with enthusiasm, her pink unicorn backpack bobbing with each step. Turning around, she sends me a joyful wave goodbye. Her smile is so bright and infectious, it lifts the weight off my shoulders.

"Have an amazing day, Myra," I call after her. "I'll see you this afternoon." For now, at least, the previous anxiety seems to dissipate.

Before I leave, I give a quick heads up to her teacher

about Myra's current situation. Once the school drop-off is complete, I have to start the most important task: finding a new nanny.

I don't think I have the strength to handle a sweet little girl who needs a lot of emotional support, while still finding a way to avoid her father. Even though I came to their rescue today, I'm not exactly a superhero.

Chapter Seven

Tyberius

STEPPING into the crisp chill of the arena from the cozy warmth of home, a blend of comfort and anticipation settles over me. The unique sound of the rink—the scrape of skates, the distant thud of pucks, the muffled calls of players—fills the air, grounding me in the reality of the day ahead.

Hockey was the constant in a childhood of variables, beginning at age six in the Rhode Island Club for Underprivileged Kids. For me, it was a lot more than a game. It was my lifeline, a way to channel energy and emotion when life at home became too much. A way to get snacks and food when my mother didn't have money or chose to buy booze instead of feeding me. It also gave me a sense of belonging and direction during those hard years.

I spent so much time perfecting my game that opportunities opened—private clubs wanted me on their roster, leading to coveted scholarships. Then recruitment from high schools and eventually the full ride to play college hockey. The cherry on top was being able to play professionally. Making a living of the one thing that might've saved my life while growing up.

Stepping into the locker room transports me back through those formative years as I don my gear. The rest of the world narrows to my singular focus—preparation and leading this team ahead. I change quickly, the ritual as familiar as breathing.

With my armor in place, I stride out of the locker room, the sounds of the rink growing louder, more insistent. The sharp scent of the ice, mixed with the faint aroma of rubber and steel from the equipment—I'm home.

Jude Decker is there by the edge of the rink, tablet in hand, next to the coaches. Probably making notes for tomorrow's game.

"Jude," I call out as I reach him.

"Ty, I'm glad you could make it on time," he states. "I take it Indie arrived at your house as requested."

"Indie?" I furrow my brow and then I remembered the woman from the relocation team telling Myra her name was Indie. "Yeah, Indigo Walker arrived earlier than I expected."

He arches an eyebrow, his piercing blue eyes glinting with amusement. "Right, Indigo Walker. I hope you're happy with this temporary arrangement. You couldn't ask for better. Myra is in very capable hands."

I nod. "Though I do trust you, I'm wondering if you had run a background check or . . ." I shrug, my shoulders tense. "No offense, I'm sure your employees are trustworthy, but as a single dad I can't take any chances."

"I trust Indie completely," he assures me, a grin playing on his lips.

"How well do you know her?"

He rolls his eyes, "For years. You shouldn't worry about Myra."

"She's been working for you for years? I mean, she's what, like twenty-one?" I ask and regret the question right away. Who the fuck cares about her age?

You, asshole. You do because that little thing isn't just pretty, she's . . . keep those thoughts buried. You're a single dad who can't afford fucking things with the only person who can care for your child.

"Twenty-six," he corrects and laughs. "You should mention to her that she looks like she's barely eighteen. She hates it." The wicked grin of satisfaction reminds me of his earlier comment. How he's enjoying making this woman the nanny.

I frown. "I take it you two know each other well."

"Really well. She's also my confidante. Which is why I know your daughter is in good hands," he assures me. "Don't worry about it."

"It's just . . . I like to have everything under

Ice, Love, & Other Penalties

control," I admit, watching a rookie execute a drill with more enthusiasm than accuracy. "Not knowing her exact qualifications or if she'll be able to find someone full time is somehow unnerving."

Jude chuckles. "Ty, if there's one thing I've learned, it's that control is just an illusion, especially when it comes to family. And hockey," he adds with a wink. "But it's how we adapt that counts. Indigo adapting to nanny duty. You adapting to changes off the ice. It's all part of the game."

His words strike a chord and maybe he's right. I have to learn to adapt.

I've been told that my biggest flaw is trying to control everything. But what's the alternative? I want my child to grow up in an organized household where she has a schedule and there are no surprises. Yet, there's always something going on, like a mother who didn't want her daughter or a grandmother who can only help me when it's convenient, or . . . There's always something disrupting our lives.

Glancing at Jude, I know this is way above his pay grade. He hired me to play hockey and lead the team to win games. Not to deal with my personal life. So, I say, "Well, I know I already said it, but thank you so much for helping me."

"Anytime," Jude says, clapping me on the shoulder. "Now, let's get to it. We've got a game to prepare for, and I need my captain's head in the game."

I nod and as I'm about to walk onto the ice he says, "Ty, when Indie appeared into our lives, she brightened everything. Trust that she'll find the puzzles to make your life just perfect. She always does."

I narrow my gaze. Are they in a relationship? Well,

knowing she's off-limits takes the tension between us away and I can focus more on what matters.

As I fall into the rhythm of practice, the sound of pucks against the boards, the shout of coaches, and the drills, the weight of the morning's worries dissipate. When it comes to the ice, it's easy to adapt. It's when I'm outside that's when I have trouble adjusting to . . . Well, almost everything.

Chapter Eight

Indigo

AFTER DROPPING MYRA OFF, I make my way out of the bustling school. I should really head to the office and start searching for a nanny to take over my duties ASAP. I haven't even checked the team's upcoming schedule yet, but I know they'll be traveling soon.

The thought of staying at Tyberius's house sends my mind wandering in dangerous directions again.

Probably best if I call Lyric and convince her to help care for Myra until I can find a permanent replacement.

As I step out of the school, I look across the street at the unassuming building that houses Decker Records—the recording studio where my father spends most of his days.

The structure, with its brick façade and large, tinted windows, always seemed like a fortress of sorts, a separate realm where the ordinary meets the extraordinary. Some of my favorite childhood memories were made within those walls, trailing behind my mom as she brought us kids to visit our dad. Instead of just being in Dad's office, they'd let us be in one of his studios where all the musical instruments are.

Dad, Grandpa Chris, and all the adults in my family always encouraged us to play with the instruments they owned. Learn to love them, and create something different. No limitations. Music may not course through my veins like it does for most Deckers, but I want to think that it's part of my soul.

I loved tinkering with different instruments, though never quite reaching the prodigy levels of my talented cousins. But those days, making joyful noises in the studios my grandfather built, will always be in my heart.

As I push open the heavy front door, that familiar comforting scent greets me—a mix of polished wood and lemon-scented cleaners. This is almost exactly like it was back when I was a little child. No matter how much time passes, some things remain constant in this place.

I smile to myself, remembering the countless hours I've spent here over the years. The lobby sits quietly, the

Ice, Love, & Other Penalties

only sound a soft guitar melody floating from the speakers. Dad likes to have some ambient music around. It's just another ordinary morning in this extraordinary place.

"Good morning, Indie," chirps Eloise from behind the front desk.

I wave in greeting. "Hey, Eloise. Is my dad busy right now?"

"For you? Never," she says with a wink. "Go on and head upstairs."

I make my way down the familiar wood-paneled hallway lined with gold and platinum records of the many artists recorded under Decker Records—Dad's legacy that my grandfather started decades ago. Every wall from the lower level all the way to the upstairs has some memorabilia.

Shiny platinum, golden albums, and photos portraying the musicians that have worked with the Deckers over the years, including shots of Dad, Uncle Matt, and even Grandpa looking young and vibrant.

When I reach the third floor, Dad's assistant Dory pops her head out. "Well, if it isn't little Indie," she exclaims.

I smile wryly. I suspect they call me "little" not because of my age, but my short stature among the tall Deckers.

Dory informs me Dad's in studio A before I can ask, adding she's already given him a heads-up that I'm here. I knock softly before turning the handle and poking my head inside the dimly lit room. The final shimmering notes of a guitar chord hang in the air as Dad glances up.

"This is a surprise, little one," he says, his voice rich

with warmth, the lines around his blue eyes crinkling as he smiles. He sets his guitar on the pedestal before rising up. "What brings my favorite youngest daughter here today?"

I can't help but roll my eyes in response to the familiar joke. "I am the youngest, and Mom forbids you to have a favorite," I remind him, stepping further into the room. The space is filled with vintage posters, each corner filled with instruments and recording equipment.

Dad chuckles, the sound reverberating through the studio. "Your mom forbids a lot of perfectly reasonable things. Did I tell you she's now getting on my case about bacon and cholesterol again?" He shakes his head with a dramatic sigh. "I adore my woman, but she's 'killing me, Smalls' with all these restrictions lately."

I raise an eyebrow at the movie reference. "We just want you healthy, Dad. Don't forget Grandpa Gabe's heart surgery a while back—you don't want that happening to you too, do you?"

He waves a hand dismissively. "Heart problems run in the family. Your great-grandma Janine had it too and after her surgery she lived over a hundred years. Why fight genetics? I'd rather enjoy a few more good years with my favorite vices on the side, extra cholesterol and all."

I huff, planting my hands on my hips. Arguing health with this man is impossible. "Mom's right, you're infuriating. You're lucky she loves you."

He grins. "That I am."

"So, what brings you here so early?" he asks, strumming an absent chord on his guitar. "Did you finally quit that ludicrous job with Jude and decide to go back

Ice, Love, & Other Penalties

to school? You can always go back to work for your Mom's PR and take over."

"No, actually I'm here because of *that* job," I explain with a sigh. I give him a quick rundown of my eventful morning with Myra and Tyberius.

When I finish, Dad scrubs a hand over his bearded jaw, looking concerned. "Taking responsibility for a child who isn't family . . . be careful with that, Indie. Can you find someone to take over on such short notice?"

"I'm going to call Teddy," I say, referring to my savvy cousin-in-law who owns a concierge company and knows almost everyone in the state of Washington. "She can find anything."

Dad nods. "Well, that's good at least." He strums a pensive chord. "You know what else might be good?"

I press my lips together wryly. "Let me guess—quitting on Jude?"

"It would solve a lot of potential headaches down the road," Dad says wisely. "What happens when he sells the team and leaves you holding responsibilities you never signed up for?"

"You're too harsh on him," I remind him. "Just because sometimes he seems like he's not serious about life, it doesn't mean that all those choices he makes are just to fuck around."

Dad presses his lips together skeptically. "He reminds me so much of your Uncle Matt when we were young."

I wave a hand. "And look how great Uncle Matt turned out. Amazing career, beautiful family . . . isn't that what you hope for Jude too?"

Dad sighs, shoulders slumping. "You definitely inherited your mother's compassion."

I give a wry smile. It's sweet that he always treats me like I'm their biological child and I could acquire things from them the way my other siblings do and so I add, "I'm wise like her too."

Dad chuckles, rising from his chair. "Alright, I'll stop pestering you about quitting on him . . . for today, at least." He pulls me into another hug. "Thanks for stopping by to see your dear old dad, Indie. Gotta get these hugs while I can."

I hug him one more time before I head out to start my workday.

Settling in behind the wheel, I pull out my phone and dial Lyric.

She answers all chirpy on the second ring. "Ooh, a call instead of a text? Did something juicy happen that I missed?"

I laugh tiredly. "I'd say pathetic more than juicy. But where to even start . . ."

"At the beginning, obviously," Lyric says. "I'm ready, coffee in hand, for the whole scoop."

A small, incredulous laugh escapes me as I dive into my eventful morning with all the details just like my sister likes it.

"So let me get this straight. Somehow, Jude roped you into taking care of this little girl named Myra."

I sigh. "Yeah, just temporarily until I find a permanent nanny situation."

Unsurprisingly Lyric laughs either at me for being so naïve or my brother for overpromising things to his players. "Classic Jude, dragging you along," she manages between chuckles. "But come on, there has to be more to this than just playing babysitter. You usually like children and are really good with them. What's bothering you?"

I hesitate, the image of Tyberius flashing across my mind. "Well, here's the thing . . ." I trail my voice, then clear my throat. "Myra's dad."

"You don't like him or is it the mom?" she asks.

"As I mentioned, he's a single dad. No mom in the picture," I clarify. "Just search for Tyberius Nolan Brynes. Go ahead, open your internet browser and just type his name. The man is . . . let's just say, distractingly hot."

"Ooh, do tell," Lyric says eagerly. "On a scale of one to spilling-scalding-coffee-on-myself-because-I'm-ogling, how hot are we talking?"

"Definitely might cause third degree coffee burns," I confess with a blush and small laugh.

I might not be fair to him. There's a lot more so I add, "He's the whole package—we're talking tall, rugged, carefree yet deliberate style. And don't even get me started on his muscles or the fact he's an athlete." I fan myself dramatically. "Let's just say Tyberius Brynes is a walking, talking distraction I do not need in my life right now."

There's a brief pause of silence before I hear Lyric's snicker through the phone. "Mm-hmm, sounds like you really, really like him, Indie. But hot single dads don't just come as eye candy—there's also a kindergartener attached."

I exhale loudly. "Of course, total no-go zone. I know better than anyone that older men, especially hockey players, are bad news." The words slip out before I can censor myself and to save face I add, "More so if there are children involved."

"That's not the statement I expected to hear," she says, concern in her voice. "Have you . . . have you been with another hockey player before?"

I wince. "It was nothing serious," I mutter evasively. "One of my hookups as usual."

No one in my family knows what happened with Frederick. No one. I feel ashamed of telling them what I did. If I hadn't been throwing myself at him . . . and then to top it all I had to quit school because I was having panic attacks during classes. Other times I would freeze in the middle of the coffee shop or the bookstore.

Some of my cousins lived there and would come to help me, but it became impossible to live alone. Mom and Dad took me home. The therapist told them I was probably not ready to live in another state away from my family or handle the responsibilities of a college student. There was also the possibility that I was burnt out thrown in mix. I worked really hard during high school, they assumed I was probably too tired to continue.

Statistics about successful high schoolers not being able to function outside a well-established routine were brought to their attention. I not only let them believe that all of it was true. I convinced myself that was the only reason why my anxiety was out of control.

Right after, I started working odd jobs for my family. Everyone had something for me. Once I had saved enough money, I moved out of my parents' house. It gave the illusion that I was fine and that nothing, nothing shakes me up. The anxiety is gone, it was just a child missing her family. The truth is that the night terrors are still there and sometimes I'm leaning against one of the walls of my house trying to calm down.

"Uh-oh, I searched this Brynes guy and just spilled coffee down my shirt. Literally," Lyric exclaims. "No wonder you're so flustered—I'd probably drop my panties if he so much as winked at me."

I roll my eyes but huff a small laugh, relieved when she doesn't press about the hockey dude I hooked up with. "So now you see my problem."

Lyric's laughter fills the car once more. "Well, you should charge Jude a lot for babysitting this guy's adorable daughter. Also, make sure those fees include a 'distraction tax' for dealing with the *hot as fuck single dad.*"

I chuckle. "Oh, I fully plan to invoice with a lot of surcharges including emotional distress."

"Still, you haven't told me who the other guy was," she circles back to that.

I groan, banging my head against the steering wheel.

"You thought I would forget." she scoffs. "I don't think so. I bet it explains your whole 'triple f' dating strategy nowadays."

"My what? Triple f?" I ask confused.

"'Fun, fuck, fly' dating strategy," she responds. "You know, having fun little trysts but no real relationships. I'm not shaming you, but it's weird that you of all people avoid getting attached."

"Me of all people?"

"For the girl who still tears up watching cute pet adoption videos? And watches rom-coms every single night. The one who bonded with everyone back in high school? Yeah, it's odd," she says frankly. "You haven't dated seriously since that cutie Justin during your sophomore year. What happened, Indie?"

"Justin was a really nice guy," I say with a small, wistful smile. We went out for a few months and then he moved to Arkansas or somewhere around the south. It's been so long I can't remember exactly where he went.

"Okay, so what happened after him?" Lyric presses. "Something must have made you shy away from dating."

I exhale, gripping the steering wheel. "I'd really rather not get into ancient history, Lyr. It was a long time ago and it doesn't matter anymore."

"If it still affects how you approach relationships, then it does matter," Lyric says gently. "But I won't push you to share before you're ready. Just know I'm always here when you want to talk, okay?"

"Love you, Lyr."

"Love you too," she replies. "And clearly being around Mr. Hunky Hockey Dad isn't good for your peace of mind. I'll meet you at your office as soon as I can and we'll sort out a replacement ASAP."

"Thank you for being the best sister ever."

Lyric just laughs. "That is what big sisters are for," she states. "I might check on Harper to see what she's doing. Three heads are better than one."

"Three it is," I agree. "I'll even pick up some pastries."

And just like that, my problems might get solved before lunchtime. It pays to be one of the youngest in my family.

Chapter Nine

Indigo

AN HOUR LATER, I'm at the new offices of the Seattle Sasquatches, perched at the edge of my desk. Harper and Lyric are cozily squished together on the small love seat across from me, laptops precariously balanced on their knees.

We're on a mission to find the perfect nanny for Myra. Someone who's not only skilled but also compassionate and loving. I mean this little girl moved across the country with her dad leaving everything behind—family and friends included. We all agree that whoever gets the job will provide stability and a sense of security to this little one.

Scanning the list with sharp eyes, Harper thoughtfully tucks a chestnut strand behind her ear. "They'll need ample experience of course, plus endless energy to keep up with a five-year-old . . ."

Lyric nods enthusiastically, "Oh, yes, stamina is a must when chasing a little one around."

Harper's gaze narrows, zeroing in on the most critical qualification. "And most importantly, someone who can handle Tyberius's rather . . . imposing personality."

Lyric snorts in amusement, flipping her hair over her shoulder flirtatiously. "By 'handle Tyberius's personality,' you mean someone who won't turn into a puddle of want every time he walks into the room with that gorgeous face." Her manicured fingers dance rapidly across the keyboard and she lifts the screen, displaying a photo of the chiseled single dad. "I mean, the man is walking artwork."

"Ten out of ten," Harper agrees with a dramatic sigh, brushing back her chestnut waves. "Even I would have trouble keeping my hands away and I swore off men long ago."

I can't help but laugh, leaning back in my chair and tapping a pen against my lips. The image of Tyberius, with his effortlessly styled hair and those green piercing eyes that seem to see right through you, flits across my mind. I release a breath, meeting my sisters' amused gazes. "Yeah, 'artwork' is one way to put it. But little

Myra needs stability right now, not a revolving door of swooning nannies."

Lyric bursts into giggles. "Oh, yes, just one smoldering look from that smoking hot hockey stud and they'd be melting into dreamy puddles under his skates."

"So true," I say.

"We'll have to find someone tough as nails who is immune to sweaty athletes." Harper winks dramatically. "Good luck with that."

That reminds me that this is serious business and I have to find someone now for my own sanity. "I know you find this amusing but we really need to find someone suitable."

Harper clicks on a profile, her expression morphing to one of concentration. "Here's a prospect. Alessia Stanley. Former preschool teacher, five years of nannying experience with high-profile families." She scans further down the page. "And it says here that she's looking for a long-term position."

Lyric leans in, squinting at Harper's screen. "Impressive. But does she know what she's signing up for? I mean, it's not just Myra. It's the whole 'dealing with the schedule of a hockey player who might be gone for days at a time.'"

"Ugh, dealbreaker. She doesn't do live-in arrangements or overnights," Harper interjects with a frown, brushing back her wavy chestnut hair in frustration. Her nimble fingers fly across the keyboard as she refines the search. "Okay, let's add a filter for willingness to stay overnight when needed."

I nod slowly, setting down my pen with a heavy sigh.

Harper closes the laptop, her probing gaze meeting

mine. "Fair warning, you're not going to like my next words."

My stomach sinks. "Just tell me," I say tightly.

"Once I added that overnight filter . . ." She winces. "Zero candidates on my site."

I let out a frustrated huff, shifting anxiously as I wring my hands. "There has to be something we missed. Here, let me dig deeper . . ." I reach for my laptop. I blow out a sharp breath, willing myself to remain calm and pragmatic. "Okay, we'll expand the parameters and reconsider previous candidates . . ."

"I have one prospect," Lyric announces triumphantly. But her face falls as she scans the screen. "Oh, wait, scratch that. She only does newborns and moves on after six months." Her shoulders slump in defeat.

Harper stands from the couch, arms crossed. "Did you have any luck?"

"No one checks all the boxes," I say, shaking my head. "What about Teddy? Has she found someone yet?"

Lyric checks her phone and shakes her head, dark hair swishing. "I texted Teddy for an update. She said it'd take some time—she needs a couple days to compile the best candidates."

I blow out a frustrated breath, glancing at my watch as the alarm sounds. It's time to pick up Myra. I stand abruptly, grabbing my purse and keys. "Keep me posted if you find any promising options. But I've gotta run to get the little one now." I open my drawer to grab some cash from my jar. "After, I'm heading to the ice cream parlor and then I'll feed her lunch."

Harper cocks an eyebrow, crossing her arms. "Shouldn't you start with lunch, then dessert?"

"Oh, shush, you," I say with a dramatic wave of my hand. "After the stressful day Myra and I've had, we deserve a little pick-me-up in the form of a magical cloud of happiness, scooped up from unicorn dreams and the land of rainbow wishes, served in a cone of chocolate and joy."

Lyric grins, "Nothing better for a rough day like a heaping cone of unicorn dreams."

"I don't know how Mom came up with that, but to this day I still believe ice cream is exactly that," Harper says. "Go get your delicious unicorn dream. We'll keep looking at other websites."

"Can't argue with that logic," Lyric chuckles. "Go enjoy. We'll keep mining the web for Mary Poppins."

I hug my wonderful sisters tightly, beyond grateful for their help. "Love you both. I'll check in later." I give a little wave then head out the door.

Chapter Ten

Tyberius

The rumble of my SUV fades as I pull up to the garage. Although, I gave a hundred and ten of myself during the training session and while we watched old videos, my mind was still back at home with Myra. The image of my child stomping her feet because things weren't going well crossed my mind a few times.

Though she's not thrown a tantrum in awhile, I

Ice, Love, & Other Penalties

worry this disruption could cause a setback. She's a good kid. No, she's great. But transitions are hard at this age.

Stepping inside, I stop short. There, in the living room, Myra sits cross-legged on the floor, puzzle pieces spread out on the coffee table in front of her, brow furrowed in concentration. It's the stillest I've ever seen her.

My gaze drifts, almost of its own accord, to Indigo. She's right next to Myra. There's a grace about Indie, an ease that belies the complexity of simply being in this space, in this moment. She's beautiful, yes, but it's more than that. It's the way she interacts with Myra, with the space around her—she seems to weave a sense of calm into the very air.

Indigo's hair catches the light, framing her face in a way that highlights her features, soft yet striking. There's an intelligence in her eyes, a warmth that seems to invite conversation without a word being spoken. Watching her, I'm struck again by an intense attraction. An involuntary pull toward her that I hadn't anticipated.

She looks up, perhaps sensing my stare, and our eyes meet. There's a flicker of something—recognition, maybe, or the spark of something new and undefined. In that single glance, there's an entire conversation we haven't had yet, a depth of interaction that goes beyond the casual exchanges we've shared up to now.

My pulse quickens as I clear my throat. "Hey, how's it going here?"

Smooth, real smooth, asshole. Why must I sound like a bumbling fool whenever I address her? Something about this woman short-circuits my brain signals and scatters my thoughts.

"Daddy," Myra jumps up from the puzzle, bouncing over to me. I sweep her into my arms, twirling her as she giggles.

"How are you, pumpkin?"

"I had ice cream before lunch," she whispers loudly. "Well, it was fluffy clouds from unicorn dreams."

"So much for let's keep it between us." Indie chuckles.

"Oops." Myra's eyes go wide. "It's okay because Indie's my new best friend."

"I see." I glance toward Indigo. "Looks like you've made quite the progress."

Indigo tucks a lock of hair behind her ears. "I think I need some notes, but overall, we've had a great day so far."

Oh, right, I promised I would forward Myra's schedule and meal plans. Before I can tell her that I'm still waiting for Gemma to email me that info, Myra says, "Indie's helping me with a big puzzle."

I nod, acknowledging my daughter, my eyes lingering on Indigo a second longer than necessary before shifting their focus to the puzzle. "I can see that. It seems like a difficult one."

Indigo's response is a nod and a smile that transforms her face into something even more captivating. It sends an unexpected flutter through my chest. I close my eyes briefly hoping it passes quickly. This attraction for her isn't something I should be experiencing.

"It's something I believe she could do," she says, as if justifying herself.

"Join us, Daddy," Myra says, tugging at my hand

with a determination that allows no argument, guiding me toward the coffee table.

As I settle cross-legged on the floor to join them, I'm acutely aware of Indigo's presence. It's only been hours since she stepped foot into this house, but so far, she has brought a sense of balance and harmony I hadn't fully realized we were missing.

We work on the puzzle quietly, the silence warm and comfortable. I find myself hoping, perhaps foolishly, that this feeling, this unexpected rightness, is just some reaction to the Washington air and it leaves soon.

Just focus on the puzzle, Brynes.

And I do. The edges of the cardboard fit together with a satisfying click, and every time I get it right, my gaze instinctively flicks to Indigo.

This time though, she's hunched over, fingers moving gracefully, sorting through the colors and shapes strewn across the coffee table. Her focus is so intense, her brow furrowed in concentration as if the world outside this puzzle ceases to exist.

Myra pouts when the piece she's trying to set doesn't fit. "Maybe this is wrong," she mumbles, frustrated.

Indie picks up a piece. "Look at this one, Myra," she murmurs, her soft voice sends an unexpected shiver down my spine. "See how this shade of blue in the corner matches our piece?"

Myra nods.

Indie hands it to her. "Also, the edges are very similar. Try to set it there."

"Got it, Indie." My daughter's enthusiasm bubbles over as she slams the piece into place, not quite as gently as Indigo would have done but with a gusto that makes both of us smile.

There's something about the way Indigo interacts with Myra, a natural ease that comes from somewhere deep within her. It's as if she radiates a warmth that reaches out, wrapping around my little girl, comforting both of us in ways I hadn't anticipated.

I lean back against the couch, arms crossed as I try to calm my body's reaction. This shouldn't be happening. Not now, not with her. The fluttering in my chest disagrees vehemently with the logic in my head. And my fucking dick . . . Well, it's ready for a lot more than just looking at the beautiful woman in my living room.

Indigo is a breath of fresh air, but she's not mine to breathe in—not permanently. Not as close as I wish.

"Dad look, we got another piece in."

"Myra, you're like a wizard of puzzles," I comment, trying to keep my tone light, casual.

Indie flashes me a grin, and I swear the room brightens a fraction. "Keep practicing and you'll be able to do those thousand-piece puzzles we saw at the bookstore."

"Are you an expert?" I ask.

She shrugs one shoulder. "My siblings and I spent rainy days lost in jigsaw worlds."

"Rainy days, huh?" I repeat.

"Yep, it was either puzzles, getting lost in books, or the music studio," she replies, turning her attention back to the task at hand.

Books and puzzles—safe topics. Though a music studio . . . who has that at home? Should I ask her more about it? No. Even discussing that feels like treading into dangerous territory. It'll mean getting to know more about her. That's not what you do with an employee. You keep things professional, so the lines are never blurred.

You, fucking liar. Gemma shared a lot about her and not once did you think about kissing her.

Kissing Indie isn't the only thing I would want to do. With Indie . . .

I want to taste a lot more than her lips.

I want to taste her all.

I want to immerse myself in the essence of her being, to explore every nuance that makes her uniquely herself. To understand her not just through words, but through the silent language of touch, the exchange of breaths, the meeting of souls.

Whoa, where did that come from? Just stop. Stop that train of thought and just make casual talk. Keep it simple and pray that she's here for only a few days.

"Books are good," I say, my voice betraying a hint of the tension knotting my shoulders. "They say they can take you anywhere." Indigo adds.

"Anywhere but here," I mutter, thinking that's exactly what I need right now.

I have no business looking at this beautiful woman. She's too young, and I . . . I am a man with many responsibilities, by a past that threatens to overshadow any chance of a future that includes laughter and lightness.

Indie nibbles on her lip, an action seemingly pure yet charged with implications that whirl my mind into a frenzy. The way in which her hair cascades over a shoulder, revealing the gentle arc of her neck as though daring me to explore its contour with a touch, with my mouth—it drives me to . . . Fuck.

I just can't seem to control my thoughts. What's the matter with me?

She's only temporary, I remind myself, a mantra meant to shield me from an inevitable crash. I can't just proposition the . . . Wait, what does she exactly do for the team?

It doesn't matter. She's the nanny and I work for her. That's plenty of reasons for me to keep myself in check.

But the more I repeat myself to behave, the less convincing it becomes.

Temporary. The word thrums in my mind.

Indigo is here only for a few days.

She's too young and I don't have time.

She's only temporary, I tell myself once more, willing my body to believe it.

Fuck, Brynes, pull yourself together.

Remember that saying of not eating where . . . I can't remember the rest, but it means don't fuck where you work or you might lose your livelihood.

I watch as she shifts, her movements graceful, purposeful, yet innocent. She doesn't know she's weaving herself into our lives. The very thought should terrify me—does terrify me. Yet there's a part of me—a reckless, hungry part—that yearns to see just how close we can get before the threads unravel.

"Indigo," I start, but freeze when she looks up. Those brown eyes wide and expectant struck me with the sudden urge to close the distance between us, to savor the unspoken words on her lips.

I clear my throat, pulling back as if scorched by the mere idea. Making an attempt to calm the sudden flare of desire. It takes more than a few beats before I manage to find my voice again. "Any luck with finding a replacement for Gemma yet?" I'm impressed at how casual I sound.

No one would know I'm having trouble controlling my body. That I need to run to the ice rink and cool the fuck down.

Indigo's brow furrows slightly in confusion. "Who's Gemma?"

"Our former nanny."

"Ah." Her reaction is subtle—a slight tilt of her head, a momentary tightening around her eyes—as she processes the information.

Since she doesn't add more to the conversation, I ask, "Were you able to interview any candidates?"

"We made several calls and searched through some of our known channels," she states, glancing at Myra. "Unfortunately, live-in nannies are hard to come by. As of right now, we have just one candidate who could cover during the day, but she wouldn't be available at night."

"If it helps, I don't expect them to actually live here," I say, keeping my tone light with some effort. "Just to be around when I can't be."

"Which means during those away games too," she states. "And that's when she wouldn't be able to be here."

I open my mouth but close it and nod.

"You sort of need a live-in nanny," Indigo states and her statement grates on my already frayed nerves, even if she's right. "As I was saying, we haven't found anyone, but I've got a lot of people on the lookout. We'll locate someone soon. I promise."

Panic spikes, hot and sharp. "I'm heading out again

next week and have a game tomorrow," I say tightly, unable to keep the tension from my voice.

"Don't worry, I'll be here for her," Indie assures me gently. "But there are a few things we should probably discuss first . . . in private." Her eyes flit briefly to Myra, as if saying this isn't a conversation for young ears.

I feel my brow furrow slightly. Does she want to discuss her living accommodations here? Could this be about a significant other? In a fleeting moment of curiosity, my gaze drifts to her left hand. The absence of a ring confirms she's not engaged or married—at least, not that I can see. A surprising sense of relief washes over me.

I mentally scold myself, *Stop it, Brynes. This isn't the time for such thoughts. Focus on what's important—figuring out what's best for your child.*

Attempting to steer the conversation back to neutral territory, I adopt a lighter tone. "If it's about choosing one of the empty rooms or deciding how to decorate it, just say the word. I'll have the relocation team get it furnished for you," I offer, paired with a playful wink. "They seem to be very responsive."

One eyebrow arches up in a sassy retort to my failed attempt at humor. "Ha, ha. Aren't you hilarious?" Indigo's response is immediate and dry, her voice devoid of amusement. "Though, I would check on that, the other thing can wait until tomorrow, during your day off."

"Sounds like a plan. In the meantime, why don't we go and get a snack?" I suggest, trying to keep the atmosphere light and friendly.

Indie's gaze shifts to her watch, a slight crease forming between her brows as she checks the time. "If it's okay with you, I have to leave."

"Why? Do you have something to do?"

She nods. "I have to pick up David and Rigby from my parents' place."

I give her a blank look, clearly not following. Does she have children? No wonder she's great with my daughter, but she's so young. And also, I wouldn't want her to leave them with someone else to care for my daughter.

Is she going to suggest bringing them? Can she take care of three children?

"You lost me—who exactly?" I admit, feeling a bit out of the loop.

"David Meowie and Rigby Barks," Indigo clarifies matter-of-factly, as if the names should ring a bell. "Though everyone in my family adores them, I think they've overstayed for today."

It takes me a few seconds to understand and actually laugh at the ingenious names of her pets. "So your dog is named after Eleonor Rigby?" I confirm since the cat is obvious.

Indie nods proudly and Myra perks up instantly. "You have pets?"

"They're more than just pets. They're my family," Indigo replies, her voice softening. She shows me her phone. "I'll text you later so we can discuss them."

And with those parting words the puzzling, beautiful woman walks away.

Chapter Eleven

Indigo

"Honey, I'm home," I call out when I arrive at my parents' home.

Nobody answers. I pull out my phone to see if they sent me a message, but all I found is one from Tyberius.

Ty: *So, are these pets an issue? Will you be able to stay with Myra or . . . it's a little concerning. Since I'm afraid of your response, I made a few calls, and my only option might be to send my child to Mom's place in Florida and believe me that's the last thing I want to do.*

My shoulders tense as I read his concerns. My fingers hover over the screen as I debate how to respond. Before I can type a reply, Rigby comes barreling toward me, tail wagging excitedly.

"Hey, buddy. Are you here on your own?" I pat his head. "Did Grandma and Grandpa leave you in charge of the house?"

"Woof." The goofy guy grins and pants. I squat to give him a good ear scratch. His tongue lolls out as he covers my face in happy puppy kisses.

I stand, glancing around. "Where's David hiding?"

Rigby tilts his head, but of course doesn't respond to me. I'm pretty sure he's trying to say, who's David and can we go home now? If we leave the feline with the grandparents, he'd be the happiest puppy in the world. My furbabies have this love, hate relationship that I'll never understand.

"Why don't we go search for him and get you a delicious treat before we go home?"

At the mention of a treat, Rigby barks and races toward the kitchen. I follow, refilling the water bowl before grabbing a cookie from the jar. Rigby gobbles it up eagerly.

"Let's go find David, buddy," I say, heading toward Mom's office where he could be hiding with Kiki. My phone buzzes with another new message. I feel a flash of irritation as I read it.

> Ty: I don't want to impose, but if you don't think you'll be able to give me a hand, I would like to know now so I can arrange . . . well, I don't even know how to get her to Florida before Monday.

I sigh before typing.

> Indie: Umm, so much for waiting until I could text you.

> Ty: I'm trying to be patient, but this is my kid we're talking about. David Meowie and Rigby Barks sound important. I'd like to discuss them, see if there will be any issues. As I said before, I may need to ask my mother for help. Which to be honest with you is worse than leaving my almost six-year-old alone at home.

I frown, trying to decide if he's kidding or if his mother is really that bad at taking care of his child. As I chew my bottom lip, considering my response, Rigby nuzzles my leg. It's pretty simple to answer Ty.

> Indie: Rig and Dave are important. They're family. They'll have to come with me when I stay overnight.

I read my reply several times before hitting send, wondering if I should disclose more. No, that's enough.

Ice, Love, & Other Penalties

I doubt he'll ask for more details. Should I tell him the truth, though?

What would Tyberius say if he knew they help quiet my anxiety? That they're the ones who keep me grounded and thanks to them I can function like a regular person.

Should I send something like, *Believe me, it's safer for your daughter if they're with me?*

Nope. It's best not to text a confession to this perfect stranger. So far, I haven't had to release that information to anyone—not even my family. Why start letting anyone in on my secret?

My friends think my attachment to them is weird enough as it is. My family doesn't judge me or think much about it. Since I was young, I dragged our pets around the house and slept with them.

> Ty: The thing is, Myra's allergic to cats.

> Indie: Lucky for you, Dave is hypoallergenic, and so is Rigby. I'm allergic to cats, too.

I smirk slightly, imagining his surprise that I've already circumvented his objection. My smirk fades though as another text appears.

> Ty: So, to confirm, you're bringing them both whenever you stay overnight? I don't know if we can accommodate that.

I blow out a long breath. How much resistance is he

going to put up with? I square my shoulders and type out my response.

> Indie: Actually . . . they come with me everywhere, anytime. Starting tomorrow, consider them part of the package deal.

I stare at the dancing dots on the screen, chest tightening. Either he's typing and erasing his response, or he's messaging Jude to complain how I'm making this too difficult. I gnaw my bottom lip. I hope he doesn't drag my brother into this. Jude's fine with me bringing the boys to the office, he even set up beds for them. But I've never outright called them a necessity before.

This might be a disaster.

My breath starts coming faster and my pulse spikes as scenarios play through my mind. What if Tyberius causes problems with Jude? What if Jude begins to look too closely into what's happening to me . . . Then he'll let our parents know and they'll be disappointed in me. I don't want them to worry about me, to see how broken I still am.

What if my entire family finds out that I'm still not okay? I repeat several times in my mind.

What if?

The walls of the room seem to bend inward as I struggle to pull in enough air. I can feel the panic attack creeping up on me, threatening to overwhelm my crumbling defenses. My skin grows clammy with cold sweat.

Then David is twining urgently around my wobbling legs, letting out plaintive mews. I sit on the floor trying to control my breathing. Rigby whines and butts his head hard against my trembling hands, big brown eyes pleading. I focus on burying my fingers deep into Rigby's warm and silky fur, using the sensations to anchor myself against the rising tide of anxiety. David's insistent purr and the solid, living weight of their bodies crowd out the crashing waves in my mind.

Gradually, my constricted lungs remember to expand. The room rights itself again. "Good boys," I murmur, as I kiss each of their heads. By the time Ty's response appears, I've regained my balance. I take a deep breath and pick up my phone again.

> Ty: Are they well trained? I've heard some animals don't like to be around kids.

> Indie: Let's start with, David and Rigby aren't animals—they're my furbabies. They're well trained to be around people and adore children.

> Ty: What if Myra gets too attached to them?

> Indie: This would be an amazing learning moment for her. She can have friends that doesn't mean they'll live with her forever.

> Ty: She keeps asking for a pet. We're not prepared for that.

> Indie: If this is a problem, I . . . I can fly her to Florida this weekend.

Not that I want to fly, but I'm certain that I can convince my sister to come along. We can call this 'a girls' trip.'

> Ty: My mother's house isn't a safe place for her. I guess I'll take my chances with your pets.

> Indie: May I ask why your mother is a bad option?

> Ty: I'd rather not disclose the issue. My mother doesn't know how to raise children.

> Indie: You seem to be okay.

> Ty: I fake it well.

My fingers hover over the screen. Should I ask him why? No, better not to push. He can keep his secrets as long as I keep mine.

> Indie: Why don't I bring them over tonight, so they get to know Myra—and vice versa?

> Ty: I guess . . . I feel like I'm doing something stupid by agreeing with your request.

> Indie: Ha, maybe I'm being the stupid one for being someone I'm not—nanny isn't in my job description.

Ice, Love, & Other Penalties

> Ty: Where are they going to sleep when you stay overnight?

> Indie: With me, obviously.

I sit cross-legged on the floor, phone resting in my lap. David is on my lap, circling before settling down with a squeaky yawn. Rigby flops down next to us with a contented huff. I scratch behind both their ears absently as I await Ty's response.

The typing bubble appears and disappears several times. I hold my breath.

I bite my lip, wondering if he'll rescind the offer. I shouldn't care if he does, but if he's right and his mother is not a good person I don't want Myra to go to her.

> Ty: Well, you'll have to order the furniture and choose the room.

I let out a relieved sigh, making David's ears twitch.

> Indie: Got it, I'll probably be at your home with my cousin to figure out what we need.

> Ty: Will you be able to have the furniture here by Monday?

> Indie: Yep. That's why Teddy is coming with me. She has a concierge business that performs miracles. It won't be cheap, but I'll make sure they bill you directly.

> Ty: Fine, are you coming tomorrow morning?

> Indie: You haven't sent me your schedule just yet, but I know there's no training tomorrow.

> Ty: Gemma used to come every day regardless of my whereabouts.

> Indie: So you'll be there tomorrow morning, but you just want me to handle the tasks to get Myra to school?

> Ty: Yes. Today is the first time I tried and you saw how unsuccessful it was.

> Indie: Okay, here's a refreshing idea. You practice getting her to school and bond with your child. I'll see you tomorrow evening, before you have to go to the arena. :wink: emoji

> Ty: That's not how this works. I'm paying you to work and do everything that involves my daughter.

> Indie: Funny that you mention it, but currently, I'm doing this as a favor—no one is paying me. And as a favor to Myra, I'm letting you learn how to be an even better father. You're welcome.

I grin down at David and Rigby. "We won and averted yet another crisis." I swear Dave gives me an annoyed look and closes his eyes while Rig wags his tail.

"Hopefully Ty and Myra will handle the invasion well enough," I mumble, trying to stand up so I can pack these guys in the car and go home.

Though, I'd love to see my parents. This is not the best time for that. I'll just leave a note and see them over the weekend.

Chapter Twelve

Tyberius

The morning in Seattle rolls in with what many say is the usual mix of drizzle and fog, just another day where the sun seems to hit the snooze button. I know I used to complain about Florida. The constant sweating and unending sun, but now. I think I miss it all.

Waking up to the sound of rain against the window is becoming my new normal. It sets a certain kind of

Ice, Love, & Other Penalties

slow-paced mood that makes me want to stay in bed just a bit longer.

Not that I can do it. Myra has to head to school, and I need to start my daily workout.

I get out of bed and head straight to Myra's room, wishing Indie was here to help us with her clothes and maybe her hair. The videos she sent me last night weren't enough to teach me how to make her hair beautiful like a princess.

Opening Myra's bedroom door gently, I see her there, asleep, completely oblivious to the world outside. "Myra," I say, not too loudly, hoping to ease her into waking up rather than jolting her awake. "Time to get up, kiddo."

She stirs a bit, one of those half-asleep, half-awake moments where you know she's trying to decide whether to go back to dreaming or face the day. I can't blame her; I feel the same most mornings.

"Daddy?" Her voice is the softest murmur, thick with sleep.

"Morning. Are you ready to start the day, sweet pea?" I offer a hopeful smile to ease her day.

"Five more minutes," Myra's voice is still thick with sleep as she sees me standing there, a break from our usual weekend-only mornings together.

"Sorry, but it's time to leave the bed and get dressed, pumpkin." I try to make my tone encouraging, but not overly pushy.

She blinks the sleep away, slowly swings her legs out from under the covers, and pads over to her closet. That's when I spot it—the favorite yellow dress she's reaching for. It's more suited for a sunny day in the park than a rainy walk to school. Before she even holds it up, I know where this is heading.

"I wanna wear this one, Daddy," she declares, pulling the dress out with enough enthusiasm that I fear she might break into a song like a cartoon princess. "With my sparkling sandals."

The dress is adorable, just like my child. But definitely not something she should wear. Not with the weather we're having today. Kneeling to her level, I prepare myself for a bit of a battle. "Looks like it's pretty wet and chilly out today. How about we pick something different, warmer, and you can rock that dress another day? We could even make it a special outfit for a special event. Maybe a fancy dinner?" I suggest, hoping we can compromise and go get breakfast.

She looks from the dress to the window, weighing her options. I can tell she's considering it. But suddenly she shakes her head. Myra smiles and clutches the dress close to her body. "I really want this one," she insists, giving me a challenging glare.

I try to recall the way Indie convinced her to wear appropriate clothes for the weather without having a big argument.

"How about this," I ventured cautiously, "you can wear the dress, but we add some layers—like leggings and a sweater over it. It's cold and rainy, and we don't want you to get sick, right?"

Myra gives me that look, holding tight to her dress, her stance all set for a standoff. "But I just wanna wear this," she shoots back, her voice edging up. I can see the tantrum brewing just behind her eyes. "If we were in Florida, you'd let me."

Hearing that makes me feel like a failure. Did I make a mistake when I decided to come to Seattle? It seemed like a solid choice. The private school she's going to is one of the best in the country. The contract I signed is worth millions and I'm thousands of miles away from my mother. This time I know she won't ask me to relocate her with us—since it seems I chose a shitty place to live.

"Listen, we're in Seattle and we both need to adjust to the changes," I state as calmly as I can. I don't even know how to sound sweet, but I hope I can muster something. "I miss Florida, just as much as I miss Winnipeg surprisingly, and . . . Well, all the states I lived in since before you were born. But it's okay because I know the new place will be just as amazing, even when it's different."

She crosses her arms and lifts her chin. "I don't like it here."

The negotiation feels more like a high-stakes diplomacy than a morning routine. "Look, pumpkin, I promise to take you to more places, so you learn to like it. For now, we have to focus on getting you ready for school and wearing the dress alone isn't an option today." I pause and head to her closet where I grab a sweater and then find a pair of black leggings in her drawers. "But wearing it with leggings and your sweater? That's like being a superhero who's ready for anything. Super Myra, brave enough to face the rain and still shine. How about that?" I tried to infuse my voice with as much excitement as possible.

There's a beat where everything hangs in the balance, then I see her grip on the dress relax a bit. "Can I pick the leggings and sweater?" she bargains.

Myra points at the ones I pulled out. "Those are ugly."

"Yes, of course," I say, sighing with relief and putting them back where they belong. "You can choose any leggings and sweater you want."

Picking out the layers turns into its own saga. She wants fall colors because fall is coming and she wants to match with the pumpkins. Fortunately, I found an oversized sweatshirt from last Halloween that she got from . . . Well, I can't even remember. And unfortunately, she can't find leggings that look pretty so she keeps the black ones. She does make me promise that I'll give Indie money to buy her new outfits for tomorrow.

At least, we find our middle ground. Watching Myra spin around, happy as can be in her layered outfit, feels like a win. All the back and forth? Worth it to see her smile. With the wardrobe crisis handled, our next adventure is arguably less contentious but equally important—breakfast. "Alright pumpkin, you ready to have some scrambled eggs with extra bacon?" I throw out there, aiming to keep the peace rolling.

Her mood flips completely at the idea, any leftover grumps gone. "Yes, can we have strawberries too?" she chimes in.

"Sounds like a plan. Strawberries it is," I agree, and we head down to the kitchen. Moving from her room, down the stairs into the kitchen feels routine, it's nothing compared to the battle we just had, I just hope that when we start preparing the food she doesn't change her mind.

The kitchen looks perfect, just like we left it last night. I pull out what we need from the fridge—eggs, bacon, and spot the strawberries on the counter. Myra drags the small stool and sets it by the counter. I hand her the whisk. "I think you're ready to be on egg cracking and whisking duty."

She straightens her back and smiles at me. "Okay. Indie taught me how yesterday."

Myra carefully taps the first egg on the edge of the bowl. It cracks open perfectly, no shell bits in sight, and she beams up at me, proud. "I did it. You should take a picture of me and send it to Indie."

"You sure did," I praise her, as she cracks another, getting ready to whisk them together. I snap a quick picture with my phone for later and begin to put the pans on top of the stove.

Soon enough I've got bacon strips sizzling away in the pan, the kitchen filling with that unbeatable breakfast aroma.

"Eggs are all whipped and ready," Myra reports proudly, offering up the bowl.

I sprinkle in some pepper, salt, and a splash of milk, giving it one final whisk for good measure. Once they hit the pan, I turn the heat down low to keep things moving slow. Gotta wait for that bacon to crisp up perfectly first before we dive in. After both are plated, we tackle the fruit course—washing and slicing strawberries together. Well, Myra washes and I cut.

Before we know it, we're eating fluffy eggs, bacon brittle, and fresh sweet strawberry slices. We grab our seats and Myra dives into her plate right away.

Seeing her so happy, I can't help but smile and think this is worth sharing with Indie. I grab my phone and shoot her a quick text with the picture of Myra cracking the eggs. After all, she's the one who said that this would be a favor to me, and I think it was.

> Ty: You wouldn't believe the negotiation standoff I had with Myra this morning over her outfit choice. It's turned into a summit about weather-appropriate clothing versus summer dresses. Plus she convinced me to give you money so you can buy her leggings because she only has ugly colors.

Almost instantly, my phone buzzes with Indie's reply:

> Indie: She does like her dresses and skirts. How'd you manage to smooth things over?

> Ty: It was a pretty tough negotiation, but I can say layering for the win. Also, I need to take her to some fancy place where she can wear just the dress.

> Indie: So you bribed her with dinner and clothes. Wow, I don't know what to say. I mean you did win, but did you? I'll see what I can do with the leggings. And don't forget to do her hair into a pretty updo.

> Ty: You're killing me here, Indie. What if I find her a hat instead?

> Indie: Nope, this is the last thing you have to do. Think of it as a quest. To finish it you have to fix her hair and take her to school.

Ice, Love, & Other Penalties

> Ty: What's my prize?

> Indie: The satisfaction of knowing you spent quality time with your child. Those are moments she'll cherish when she's older. I still remember those days when Dad would braid my hair before school and drive me and my siblings along.

> Ty: I guess that's something I've never considered. It's so hard to do it during the season.

> Indie: You can always find the time. Now, I'm going to continue enjoying my morning tea before I start my day.

> Ty: Fine, but we're seeing you later today, right? I have a game.

> Indie: I'll be there, don't worry about it.

But I'm pretty concerned. Not that she won't come, but that I'm smiling like an idiot after putting down the phone.

Chapter Thirteen

Tyberius

Myra's soft snores drift from her room as I pace the living room like a caged tiger. Tonight's game—a victory for the Seattle Sasquatches—should have been the highlight, a reason for celebration, yet my mind is elsewhere.

My thoughts are consumed with Indigo Walker—

Ice, Love, & Other Penalties

stubborn, maddening, bold and beautiful Indigo Walker who insisted on driving all the way to her brother's place by herself—at this time of night.

I admire her independence, her fierce spirit, but she clearly doesn't understand the concept of self-preservation. And then, there's the attraction I feel toward her. We just met yesterday morning and her beautiful face keeps popping in my mind more often than it should.

What is it about Indigo Walker that draws me in?

I try distracting myself with game highlights, but my thoughts keep drifting back to Indigo. Her laughter, the passion lighting her eyes when she's animated about something. She pulls at me like a gravitational force I'm helpless against.

Worst of all, I can't shake this fierce protective instinct. Its intensity unsettles me. I'm not used to feeling this way, yet I can't deny its power.

There's something below the surface. Something she hides from the rest of the world. And maybe the fact that she has to be around her pets is not because she's attached to them. I didn't pry earlier, but perhaps there are deeper reasons she keeps them close.

Is she sick? I want to believe that Jude recommended someone who's capable, but what if he hid something that's important? It's not too late to take a plane to Florida tomorrow to drop Myra off with Mother before my trip.

Before I can think better of it, I'm dialing Jude. Fortunately, he picks up on the second ring.

"Another emergency, Brynes?" comes his dry voice.

I grip the phone tighter. "Are you certain Indigo can handle staying overnight with Myra?" I blurt out.

"You'd tell me if . . . if there were any issues I should know about?"

He scoffs through the line. "Yes, she is. And though I meant it when I said we're here to help, isn't it late for house calls?"

He might be right, but . . . I scrub a hand down my face. "She brings a dog and cat everywhere . . ." I trail off, unsure how to voice my doubts.

"Dave and Rig?" Jude scuffs. "Mom says they have better manners than me. What's the problem there?"

"Why does she bring them everywhere?" I ask, a little confused about why his mother knows the animals.

"Fuck if I know. It's just her quirk." I can almost hear his shrug. "We never questioned it, even when she was little."

I halt mid-step, a nagging thought hitting me. "Exactly how do you know Indigo?"

"Indie is my baby sister," comes his casual reply.

"Fuck," I mutter under my breath. Perfect, just too fucking perfect. Of course, I would be attracted to the boss's sister. Yet, another reason to keep my distance from the far-too-tempting Indigo Walker.

I clear my suddenly dry throat. "She said her name was Indigo Walker . . ."

Why is it that I don't want him to be related to her? Because he's yet another layer as to why I should stay away from her.

"Well, it's technically Walker-Decker. She drops the Decker though. My sister hates the spotlight."

His nonchalance only sparks more questions, but I simply mutter a vague thanks and end the call before I dig myself deeper. Attraction or not, Indigo Walker—or should I say, Decker—spells nothing but trouble.

Against my better judgment, I message Indigo directly instead of admitting I informed Jude about her solo drive home.

> Ty: Did you make it home?

A reply bubbles up instantly.

> Indie: No. I told you I was heading to Gabe's place. We're having a family sleepover. I think it's my sister's way to ask for help with our niece and nephew. She's great with them but hates to babysit alone. Though, I heard you were bitching to Jude about me.

I stare dumbly at the screen, scrambling for words.

> Indie: Dave and Rigby showed you they're well educated. Honestly, they behave a lot better than some of my brothers. What's the issue there, Brynes?

I hesitate before typing a reply.

> Ty: They seem less like pets and more . . . support companions?

The dots dance for several moments before her response.

> Indie: So you were asking Jude if I have medical problems or something?

I sigh, raking my hair back. Of course she'd see right through me.

> Ty: You need to understand that I want my daughter to be safe. What if you have something serious and she shouldn't be alone with you. She's everything to me.

> Indie: It's understandable, but my brother Gabe and my cousins trust me with their kids. I'm the best at watching the little ones. If you have questions, ask me, not my brother.

I scrub my jaw. She's right—I overstepped.

> Ty: Still, I had to look out for my daughter.

> Indie: I get it but talk to me directly next time. She's safe with me.

I type another reply before thinking better of it.

> Ty: So, you're a Decker, huh? How was it growing up with famous people?

I instantly regret prying, but her response comes too fast.

> Indie: This is why I don't share my full name. I dislike people who assume they know my family or treat me differently for it.

> Ty: My apologies, I didn't mean to overstep. It's just . . . when you grow up with Without A Compass and other Decker bands, it's hard not to wonder what that household was like, surrounded by so much talent.

I hit send before I can self-edit and backtrack. The typing bubble appears, then disappears, reappearing several times as I pace anxiously.

Finally, her message pops up.

> Indie: Makes me question if people want me for me . . . or just to get close to my famous siblings or dad.

I wince, cursing internally at sticking my foot in my mouth again.

> Indie: This is Keith—Indie's favorite cousin. Word of advice, my dude, put down the phone. You're lucky she agreed to look after your kid. Answering your question, being a Decker is fucking fantastic. Not because of the fame, but because we look after one another so . . . stay away from her and keep this professional. We are watching you.

I stare at my screen wondering if I should answer or just ignore the cousin. He's right though I shouldn't have asked about the family. What matters is that she's safe and my child is in good hands, right?

If only I could stop thinking about Indigo's kissable lips.

Chapter Fourteen

Tyberius

THE CONCEPT of morning loses all significance when Myra, my bundle of inexhaustible energy, decides it's time to start the day. Without any warning, she launches herself onto my bed, her small hands shaking me awake. "Daddy. Daddy, wake up. You promised we'd go to the park today . . . or the children's museum." Her voice, filled with anticipation and excitement, is a lot more effective than any alarm clock.

This would be perfect any other day, except, it's Saturday.

I groan playfully, feigning sleep a moment longer before blinking my eyes open to meet her shining gaze. "Is it morning already?" I ask, my voice still gravelly with sleep.

"Yes." She bounces excitedly on the bed, nearly vibrating with enthusiasm. "And you said we could go somewhere fun today if you won the game last night."

I roll pretending to go back to sleep and stifle another groan into my pillow, buying a few more seconds of dozing before I turn over with a sigh.

"Wakey, wakey," she grins. "We're having a fun day, Daddy."

This is all my fault though. I gotta be smarter offering victory-fueled rewards when winning is already part of my job description. Maybe I should start promising something different and as a reward for her good behavior at school instead.

I sit up, pulling Myra into a warm hug. "Alright, pumpkin," I say, planting a kiss on her hair. "Let's get this day started. What's the first order of business?"

"Breakfast," she says too cheerfully, then adds, "Pancakes à la Indie, with lots and lots of syrup." She rubs her belly and licks her lips for dramatic effect.

"We just had pancakes yesterday," I remind her. "And we would need Indie here to make them as yummy as hers."

"Yesterday it was eggs and strawberries." Myra crosses her arms with an exaggerated pout. "I want pancakes."

"Let's check what's in the pantry and fridge." I swing my legs out of bed. "Ready to go?"

Myra nods and I scoop her up, making airplane noises as I carry her all the way downstairs to the kitchen. She giggles and spreads her arms out like wings. Once I set her on the floor, we scan the contents of the cupboards and refrigerator. I suggest my famous poached eggs, but she scrunches her nose.

Then I say, "How about oatmeal with freeze dried fruit?" That earns me another pout from Myra.

"Okay, no eggs or oatmeal today. How about . . . fruit salad, yogurt, and cereal?"

Myra gives me a firm nod, her expression brightening. I take out the ingredients while she sets her small stool in place, ready to assist me.

"You're the best little helper in the world," I tell her warmly as she opens the cereal box and sets the two crystal bowls on the counter for the yogurt.

"Really?" She glances up at me hopefully.

I smile and nod in confirmation. Just then, the doorbell rings sharply, slicing through the cozy kitchen.

"Who's that? A delivery?" Myra's attention is instantly divided, her curiosity piqued by whoever is at our door but also by the yogurt she needs to pour into the bowls.

"I guess we'll have to find out." I rinse my hands and wipe them with a dish towel.

"Maybe it's Grandma," Myra suggests, bouncing on her toes with a sparkle of hope in her eyes.

Doubtful, I don't say. For that to happen I'd have to buy her ticket—first class, as well as bribe her with something and also pay her expenses because . . . Well,

I don't know what my mother will use as an excuse, but I know for sure it isn't her.

"It could be a surprise," I offer instead, racking my brain. Maybe I ordered something within the last couple of days and it's arriving today.

Myra slips off her stool, her small feet hitting the floor with soft thuds as she trails behind me to the door. The possibility of a neighbor dropping by to welcome us crosses my mind as I reach for the handle, but the sight that greets us sweeps away all such mundane expectations.

Indie, with Rigby by her side, stands on our doorstep. The morning's interruption suddenly transforms into a pleasant surprise in an instant. Indie looks beautiful, yet different from yesterday. Her hair is captured in a carefree bun, wispy strands framing her lovely face, highlighting her natural beauty. She's wearing a flowing purple blouse paired with ripped jeans. The simplicity of her attire only adds to her charm, making her look effortlessly adorable.

"Good morning," she says, her voice carrying the warmth of the sun that's hidden from view. Her smile, wide and sincere, lights up her face. "Hope we're not interrupting anything."

Before I can respond, Myra rushes past me, darting toward the pup. "Rigby," she exclaims, wrapping her arms around the dog who meets her embrace with nothing but patient affection, his tail keeping a slow, contented beat.

"Seems like you brought her a new best friend," I say, my eyes briefly scanning Indie's surroundings for a carrier or . . . Well, I don't know where else she'd contain her cat. Since I don't see her with the carrier I ask, "Where's David?"

Indie brushes a stray lock of hair from her face and gives a small smile. "He stayed with my cousins. Long story."

"We're about to have breakfast. Would you like to join us?" I suggest, stepping aside to welcome them further into our home.

"Sure," she replies, her voice softer now, a smile tugging at the corners of her mouth. Rigby gives an approving bark, as though seconding the motion. "He definitely agrees, though I doubt you have anything for him."

"Sorry, we don't have dog treats but if you give us a list, we'll be happy to stock our pantry with them," I say as we move back into the kitchen.

Myra turns to Indie and says. "Now that you're here, can you make pancakes à la Indie?"

"She's not here to work, pumpkin," I remind her gently, trying to temper her expectations without dimming the spark in her eyes.

Myra's bottom lip quivers ever so slightly, her big eyes shimmering with a blend of hope and calculated sadness. It's the look that has swayed me countless times before. No one, and I mean no one, can say no to this child.

Leaning against the doorframe, arms crossed, I watch the scene unfold before me. There it is—the inevitable crumbling of Indie's defenses under the sheer power of Myra's pleading gaze. Who could blame her? Those wide, hopeful eyes have a way of bending the world to their will.

Indie crouches down, meeting Myra at eye level.

"Why don't we leave that for Tuesday morning? Remember, that's when I'm coming with Dave and Rig for a sleepover."

There's a long silence after Indie's suggestion. I can almost see the gears turning in Myra's head, weighing the disappointment against the delayed gratification.

"I'm here just to check the rooms," Indie continues, straightening up and casting a brief glance my way.

In that fleeting moment, our eyes lock. There's a flash of something in her eyes, a hint of the same unsettled feeling that's been gnawing at me. For a second, I wonder if she's feeling the same pull I do or if I'm just imagining it.

But too quickly I remind myself that it's too early to have stupid thoughts about the only person who can look after my child next week. Not that I should even once I get a nanny. She's my boss's little sister. That makes her forbidden as fuck.

Indie glances at the counter and says, "Cereal and fruit sound like a good, yet, fast breakfast."

Myra's face falls slightly. "Oh, you're not coming with us to the park?" she asks, my heart squeezing at the note of disappointment in her voice.

Indie shakes her head. "No, sorry. I came to figure out which room I'll be using. Remember, Dave, Rigby, and I will be sleeping over on Monday and Thursday?" she reminds her, trying to soften the blow and offering my child something to look forward to.

"Yes," Myra claps excitedly and the disappointment is gone. "But are you sure you can't do anything today with us?"

I see now why Jude said she was the perfect candidate, and great with kids. So far, she hasn't given in to

Ice, Love, & Other Penalties

any of my child's requests and my kid hasn't had a meltdown. I should ask her to give me a few more parenting lessons. Because clearly, I suck.

"Well, I have to get the furniture," Indie explains further.

"We can come with you," Myra states then glances at me with those big eyes. "Right, Daddy?"

I rub my temples. This child is persistent no doubt. And somehow this has become a match between her and Indie. Myra is trying everything to convince her to stay or at least spend some time with us today. My money is on my child—she's the most stubborn person I've known, followed by her mother.

Indie taps her chin. "Though, that's an amazing offer. I'll have to pass. Maybe next time I decide to go shopping you can come with me."

"Okay," Myra finally lets it go.

"And since planning is my favorite thing to do, I'll try to come up with something for Monday, when we have our sleepover." The way Indie says it, perhaps unintentionally suggestive, sends an involuntary shiver down my spine, making my body tense and my cock semi-hard.

I swallow hard, battling the sudden influx of thoughts that are far too inappropriate for the moment, especially with Myra nearby. The mere idea of Indie spending the night, under my roof, stirs a turmoil within me that I struggle to suppress.

What the fuck is wrong with me? I chastise myself internally for letting my thoughts wander so recklessly.

"While you check the rooms, we'll finish setting up breakfast," I manage to say, aiming for a tone of nonchalance to mask the very inappropriate thoughts raging within me.

Indie offers me one of her sweet smiles. "Thank you, Ty. We'll probably have everything delivered by Monday after you drop Myra to school, so we don't disrupt your weekend."

The opportunity to extend the time we could spend together presents itself, and I seize it, despite what common sense dictates. "You're welcome to do it anytime, so I can help."

She dismisses the offer with a gentle wave of her hand. "I'll think about it. You two, continue with breakfast. I won't take long." Her assurance does little to ease the sudden tightness in my chest.

And now I understand why my child is being so insistent. We want to spend time with Indie. Whether it's going shopping or making pancakes, how is it that we've come to feel like we need Indie around?

As she turns to head upstairs, her voice drifts back to me, lighter now as she begins a phone call. She sounds a bit unsure and I'm wondering who she's talking to. "Yeah, I'm here to measure the room as you requested. You sure we can do this on such short . . ."

"You should tell her to come with us, Daddy," Myra suggests softly, her voice carrying a mixture of hope and a slight sense of urgency. "I really like her and Rigby."

Ah, so Myra hasn't given up yet.

Well played, kid.

Well. Played.

I want Indie to come along as much as Myra does, but I play the practical dad. "Pumpkin, Rigby can't come to the museum with us. They have rules about dogs. Let's plan something with him next time, okay?"

Myra sighs dramatically, but fortunately, she drops it.

Situation averted for now.

I hope that by next week, we might have a new nanny, and things could go back to our old normal. But there's this part of me, a part that's getting louder, wondering if 'normal' without Indie is what we really want.

Chapter Fifteen

Indigo

As I HOLD up my phone, angling it to give Teddy a panoramic view of the empty guest room. Such a waste of perfectly good space. I can't help but marvel at the prospect of creating something in here for those nights I have to stay with Myra.

"It's the one overlooking the garden, you know, with

Ice, Love, & Other Penalties

the large bay window," I explain, stepping back to allow for a fuller view.

Teddy's eyes light up on the screen, a spark of recognition flickering. "Ah yes, I remember. That room has so much potential. We could really make it sing with a bit of your flair. What are you thinking for colors?" she asks enthusiastically, rubbing her hands together.

I chew on my lip, picturing the possibilities. "I'm leaning toward something calming . . . maybe a soft lavender or a muted sage green? You know, something that would make the room feel like home," I muse, imagining the soothing hues.

Teddy nods, scribbling something down. "Perfect. Those colors will complement the natural light beautifully. And for David and Rigby? What's the plan there?" she inquires.

I turn the camera toward a cozy nook by the window. "I was thinking this spot could be perfect for David's bed. As for Rigby, maybe we can have a couple of cat trees?" I suggest hopefully. "His litter robot could go next to the private bathroom too."

Once Dave, Myra, and Ty are comfortable with each other I will ask if we can get a few more cat litters around the house.

Teddy nods thoughtfully. "As I said, I have the blueprints of that house. He didn't ask for much when we offered our services because he had his own furniture," she reminds me with a sigh.

"Why am I not surprised that he didn't ask for help? But now we're in a bind because he only furnished two of the rooms," I state with a frustrated shake of my head.

Teddy scrunches her nose. "You don't think I told him that? I sent him several proposals that included decorating the office, library, and basement. He declined everything."

"Not the library," I gasp, laying it on thick with mock horror.

"Mock me again, and you're on your own," she retorts, a smirk playing on her lips before pointing off-camera, caught up in a moment of inspiration. "You know what else we can do? We can add some shelves for David to climb on, maybe a custom pet bed that matches the room's aesthetic for Rigby. It'll be their little paradise too."

I grin, picturing the cozy nook we could create for my furry kids. "That sounds amazing. I can already see David perched up high, surveying his kingdom."

Teddy's excitement practically zips through the phone, her voice bubbling with enthusiasm. "We'll make it happen. I'll start drafting some ideas and will send them to you within the next hour so you can approve them. We'll create a space that feels like home for all of you," she promises, her voice brimming with enthusiasm. "We should have the construction crew there tomorrow. Is that okay? I don't want to bother anyone, but that's the only way to ensure that you get everything set by Monday afternoon."

I nod as I head back downstairs to the kitchen over to where Ty and Myra are setting breakfast on the kitchen island.

"Hey, Ty, do you have a second?" I ask leaning against the kitchen counter, phone in hand.

Ty looks up from pouring the cereal, a welcoming smile on his lips. "What's up?"

Ice, Love, & Other Penalties

I turn the screen so they can meet my cousin. "This is Teddy. Teddy, meet Ty and Myra."

Teddy waves enthusiastically. "So nice to put a face to the voice, Mr. Brynes. Hey, Myra, it's nice to meet you."

Ty waves, a little surprised by Teddy's greeting.

Myra peers curiously at the screen. "Hi, Teddy. Do you like rainbows?"

Teddy laughs. "I sure do, Myra."

Once the introductions are done, I explain our plan to Ty. "So, to make sure the room is ready for the furniture, we'll need a construction crew here by tomorrow so they can do some improvements."

Ty's eyebrows raise in surprise.

"I don't think it'll be more than an eight- to ten-hour job," Teddy assures him. "However, I don't want to disrupt you during the weekend. They'll be working on adding bookcases, shelves and painting the walls among other things. We're aiming to get everything set by Monday afternoon."

Myra's attention shifts from her fruit salad, visibly intrigued. "Are we painting the house?" she asks, her eyes lighting up eagerly.

Teddy chuckles. "Just the guest room, Myra. We want to make it really nice for Indie, Dave, and Rigby. How does that sound?"

Ty shares a quick concerned look with me. "Eight to ten hours seem like a long time," he says, his mouth turning down slightly. "Is there a way you could split the crew between today and tomorrow?"

Teddy taps her chin thoughtfully. "You know what, I think I can get them there around one or two if I start making some calls right now. That way they'll leave no later than six. Tomorrow, we could do . . . What works best for you?"

"Ten," he states. "We might go to brunch and do other activities."

"You can take them to brunch with your parents," Teddy suggests brightly. "Then they can move the party to the grandparents' house."

Is she fucking insane? I give her a piercing look, hoping she gets the message that that won't be happening. "They're definitely not ready for the full family experience," I state politely through gritted teeth.

"I want a family. My grandma is in Florida," Myra pipes up, her chin quivering sadly.

This poor child is breaking my heart. Although, I know my family will welcome her—you don't just bring strangers to the Deckers. They're pretty overwhelming even for me—and I'm family. I know I'm going to regret what I'm about to say, but I do it. "Why don't you drop by my place for brunch? After that we can do something fun, like the turtle sanctuary or a visit to Luna Harbor. We can take the ferry there."

"Luna Harbor is fun! You can also try Silver Lake which is a bit closer," Teddy suggests helpfully. "I'll send you some options so Myra can have a nice day out."

Myra is clapping and I'm just wondering how I'll get out of this one. So much for not interacting with Tyberius more than I need to.

We say our goodbyes and I notice Ty regarding me thoughtfully as I end the call. "Well, that was unexpected," he says wryly. "Are you sure it's okay if we swing by your house tomorrow?"

"Definitely," I say brightly, looking at my watch.

"Well, I have to leave now. My next stop is furniture shopping."

Ty's face falls slightly. "You're not spending the day with us?"

I shake my head, the lie flowing easily off my tongue. "Oh, no, I already have plans with my cousins—the ones who kept Dave. We have an entire day ahead of us." I force a regretful look, hoping he buys it. "But I'll see you tomorrow for brunch, right?"

"Wouldn't miss it," Ty confirms, though his eyes search my face like he suspects there's more I'm not saying.

I grab my things, calling out for Rig before I wave a quick goodbye and jet out of the house.

Chapter Sixteen

Indigo

I STEP into the furniture store, scanning the displays with a sense of mission: find the perfect additions for my soon-to-be new room at Ty's place.

As I wander the aisles, a twinge of doubt creeps in. Am I investing too much time and emotion into this? Lyric insisted last night that it's logical, since I'll be spending lots of time there until we find a nanny—she's skeptical that will even happen before the season ends. Jude desperately hopes I'll stay at least until June, when he's convinced the Sasquatches will win the Cup.

My poor brother thinks that they can go all the way. This has been his dream since he started playing hockey —maybe not exactly the way he originally envisioned. Since he can't play anymore, he wants to do it through his players. If living vicariously through his players keeps Jude's own dashed hopes from poisoning the next generation, I guess that's the lesser of two evils.

Keith suggested I look into an au pair agency. He dated one when he lived in New York. He can't remember where she was from—but she had a sexy accent. My cousin can only think about two things: music and the people he finds attractive enough to fuck.

The point he tried to make last night was that most au pairs live-in with the host family. I didn't really understand the arrangements well, but I made a note to research more later. Ty only wants the nanny to stay overnight when he's not home. I'm not sure if he'd be comfortable having someone live permanently in his house . . . and if we hired her, would she stay long-term?

I brush the thought aside for now, and research that early next week. I also have to check in with Ty but only if I feel it'll be good for Myra. Her earlier words about wanting a family are back on my mind. I still wonder about Ty's mom. If any of us needed someone to look after our children, Mom would drop everything to be with them. She even does it for our cousins.

As I wander through the aisles looking at the furniture and thinking about the Brynes and their family dynamic, my phone buzzes. I wonder if it's Teddy texting me her discount code or . . . I check and it's actually Ty.

> Ty: I received an email from Teddy with the list of activities we could do this weekend. Myra wants to go on a ferry ride. Would you want to go to Luna Harbor with us?

I should tell him that Silverthorne is more fun today and we could stay the night at the Luna Harbor Inn. And though the idea is great, I use it to get rid of my brunch invite for tomorrow.

> Indie: I wish I could, but I'm swamped today. I can help you by giving you not only suggestions but an itinerary. Let me gather some links.

> Ty: I thought you were going to buy furniture. We can wait until you're done.

> Indie: I'm at the furniture store already, but there are a lot more things I have to do in order to be free next week for Myra. I'll take a seat on this plush sage green sofa and prepare this for you.

> Ty: Why are you looking at a sofa? I have a perfectly good one here, no need to replace it.

Ice, Love, & Other Penalties

> Indie: I can still look at things even when I don't buy them. This one is soft and plushy and . . . it invites you to sit in with a good book and a blanket.

> Ty: Would you like me to leave you alone with the couch, seems like you two are having a . . . moment.

> Indie: Ha, you're not funny. Okay, I just sent you the links and what I think you should do there.

> Ty: You want me to stay overnight in Luna Harbor?

> Indie: That's better than coming back to Seattle and then having to drive there.

> Ty: What happened to brunch?

> Indie: We can move it to whenever you have a free weekend. I'm saving you a four-hour drive—think about Monday's game.

> Ty: True, I'll deal with Myra.

> Indie: Tell her about the lavender farm—she can harvest her own lavender or prepare soap or . . . It'll be so much fun.

> Ty: Is it safe?

> Indie: Of course it is. Do you think they'd let children participate in something unsafe?

Ty: I trust you.

> Indie: Perfect. If you can bring me some lemon-lavender tea, I'll appreciate it.

Ty: You got it. So Silverthorne first, then Luna Harbor. Got it.

> Indie: Have fun.

Ty: You too, just make sure not to add unnecessary things to the room, please. It's just temporary and I won't be having guests after you.

> Indie: Where did the nanny stay when she was working for you?

Ty: Gemma and Myra came to every away game with me—unless Myra was sick or there was an issue. If she had to stay at my place, she would use the sofa bed I have in the living room. And we planned to continue doing exactly the same.

> Indie: Why not a bedroom?

Ty: When we were in Florida, I lived in a two-bedroom townhome. I'm used to that.

Ice, Love, & Other Penalties

> Indie: But you live in Seattle and have plenty of rooms.

> Ty: I didn't think about it. We had a routine. I honestly didn't see the point in buying a bed. I don't like to spend money on frivolous objects.

Somehow, the idea of making him spend money on furnishing and decorating the room now feels wrong. What if I'm imposing? I would hate to be that person.

> Indie: If you need me to sleep on that couch, I can try.

> Ty: No, I want you to get the room set up and make it comfortable for you. Maybe that's something I should've done before we moved in. All my life I've lived on a tight budget—spending money unnecessarily makes me anxious. What if tomorrow I lose my ability to skate or play hockey? I need to know I'll have enough put away to support Myra no matter what happens. But that doesn't mean basic things like furnishing a room and providing a decent place for you to sleep is going to bankrupt me. It's just . . . I don't know, it makes me extremely anxious to think that I'll lose everything I've built. I'm not sure if there's a word for what I feel, but it's sometimes hard to handle.

> Indie: Trauma. It's called trauma. You should try a therapist. I'm not saying that your spending should change, but having anxiety for it is not good for your physical or emotional health.

Ty: Sorry, I didn't mean to dump all that on you. Please make sure you set up the space the way you feel is best. We're going to get ready to leave. Can you send a list of what Myra should wear and what she should pack, please?

> Indie: Why?

Ty: Because you're from here, and you know better than either one of us.

> Indie: So, you don't want to fight with her and it's best if you blame me when she tells you the sparkly sandals are perfect for today?

Ty: Exactly.

> Indie: She needs waterproof boots. I'll send you the address of a store in Silverthorne where you can get them. They have sparkly ones—that will be a great substitute for those fabulous sandals.

Ty: Did I make a mistake by moving here?

> Indie: Why would you ask that?

> Ty: Myra keeps wanting to move back to Florida. She doesn't seem very happy here.

> Indie: Adjusting will take time—for both of you. I suggest you just show her that she has her dad who adores her and show her how amazing it is to live here. I'm thinking that today's trip will help you both.

> Ty: I hope you're right.

> Indie: I think I am and . . . I'll make sure to schedule a playdate with my niece Cora. She's around Myra's age.

> Ty: Thank you.

> Indie: No worries. Now, I'm going to send a picture of this couch to Teddy. Maybe we can make it fit in my room.

> Ty: :rolling-eyes: emoji

After reading Ty's last message, I snap a picture of the couch, sending it to Teddy with a quick, "What do you think? Would it fit?"

Her reply is almost instantaneous.

> Indie: Love it. :smiling cat face with heart-eyes: emoji Do they have a smaller size, like a lounge chair or a love seat? What about a bookcase? I ordered the bed. It'll arrive tomorrow at Ty's house.

I send the pictures of the bookcases I saw earlier. I get another enthusiastic approval from Teddy. She sends me to another store to check out the light fixtures. My cousin wasn't kidding when she said she'd have me going around to several stores before we had the perfect room.

But does it need to be perfect?

I'm not sure, but this isn't a room just for me, but maybe for the next person who'll be staying with Myra, hopefully for several years. After my text exchange with Ty I believe that she needs a lot more than just a person to look after her, but someone who'll agree to be there for the long run. I'll make sure we'll get her that even if I have to stay until next year.

Chapter Seventeen

Tyberius

THE HOTEL ROOM is quiet except for the low hum of the air conditioner. I sink onto the edge of the bed with a wince, my left knee creaking in protest. Games like this make my thirty-six-year-old joints feel too damn old for professional hockey.

I press a cold pack to my aching left shoulder, hoping to ease the persistent pain. With my free hand, I grab my phone from the nightstand, realizing I haven't checked it since arriving at the arena hours ago. A grin tugs at my lips when I open it to find a new text from Indie. Attached is a photo of Myra all cozy in bed, sleepy-eyed but smiling, ready to drift off to sleep.

> Indie: When you read this Myra will probably be asleep, but she wanted to wish you goodnight and congratulate you on that amazing goal tonight.

I stare at my daughter's sweet face. My lips turn into a big smile, I adore my little troublemaker. Moving to Washington wasn't a mistake, but it probably wasn't the best timing. I was aware of the biggest change she would be going through. Myra had to go to school full time, so she wouldn't be traveling with me. And maybe it's something I should've done last year when she was supposed to start preschool.

Fatherhood is difficult, and fucking up is so easy. Since Saturday I've been wondering if Indie is right and if I should be reaching out to a therapist. I don't like to spend much money on . . . Well, anything. Every other minute I keep second-guessing everything I do in my life.

Moving to another team, becoming a father . . . I knew bringing her into my life would be life-altering. Becoming a father—a single father—was a bold and probably risky move for a man who spends so much time on the road and has to dedicate a lot of his time to training.

However, I've made it work, because she's worth it. This little girl changed my entire life and though we're

Ice, Love, & Other Penalties

happy together, for the past few days I've had this nagging feeling that there's something missing in our lives.

Indie's beautiful face comes to mind though.

What the fuck, Brynes? You have to stop having that woman at the forefront of your mind.

But it's almost impossible. There's something about her that makes me think crazy shit that's practically impossible. I have this urge to text her back something sweet and flirty, yet not overly suggestive.

But I stop myself. She's a woman who probably likes romance and is waiting for her happily ever after. Things I can't offer her. However, it'd be good to check on Myra.

So, I text her.

> Ty: Thanks for the pic. I can't wait to pick Myra up from school.

That's good, right? Should I have added tomorrow? Does it sound dumb?

"It's a text, not the next American novel, idiot," I mutter under my breath.

I set down the phone, content to wait however long it takes for her reply. Maybe she'll just ignore me, and I'll see her tomorrow or . . . Wednesday? I hope that I get a glimpse of her before that. A brief exchange where I can see her, hear her voice and obviously lust after her. Because it seems like it's the only thing I do when she's around.

Indie: Why don't I plan on picking her up? Just in case the flight gets delayed, or my brother thinks there has to be a meeting.

> Ty: I'm pretty sure that won't happen. Jude hates meetings. But why don't I text you if I don't make it on time?

Indie: Sounds like a plan.

I should leave it at that, but I, of course, don't know how to leave enough alone.

> Ty: How's everything going? Did she have a good day at school?

Indie: Yep, and we did some homework before and after dinner.

I raise my eyebrows in surprise.

> Ty: Kindergarteners have homework now?

Indie: Not usually, but the teacher wants her to work on her fine motor skills.

> Ty: And what exactly do you have to do?

> Indie: I brought a few games and things with me. We played Operation. Tomorrow, we'll be sorting Mom's bucket of buttons and on Friday, we'll probably bake cookies.

> Ty: And eating cookies helps somehow? (Glances skeptically)

> Indie: Yeah, you can work on her fine motor skills while decorating them.

> Ty: I'm not sure if that's educational but it definitely sounds delicious.

> Indie: And it is pretty rewarding if you like sugar.

This small talk feels strained, yet I don't want to let her go just yet. It's difficult to steer the conversation beyond Myra. I want to ask more about her. What did she study? Why is she working for the Seattle Sasquatches or . . . I just want to learn everything about her. Is that crossing a line? Probably. So, I stick to our safe topic. My child.

> Ty: But overall, she had a good day?

> Indie: Yep. She's bummed though. Dave didn't want to come out from under my bed.

> Ty: She's been wanting to hold him since the first time he visited the house.

> Indie: And she will, once he's comfortable with this place—and her. She'll have to wait until he comes to her.

> Ty: This is a good way to teach her patience, I guess.

> Indie: It's a good lesson indeed. Especially in a world of instant gratification.

> Ty: So you like to be rewarded right away too? You behave like a good girl?

I freeze as soon as I hit send, eyes wide. Did I really just flirt via text? And I swallow hard when I read her response.

> Indie: It all depends. Sometimes being on the edge of desire is better than just getting IT right away. Though, I'm not always a good girl—bad girls get rewarded too.

My mouth goes dry. Is she implying what I think? I should leave it alone, but some reckless part of me wants to nudge just a little further . . . see if she takes the bait. Sexting today. Tomorrow . . . No, I need to stop that thought. This is crossing a major line. I sigh with relief when I receive another text from her.

Ice, Love, & Other Penalties

> Indie: We got off track. But to answer your question about waiting for rewards, I can tell you that my parents taught me patience. When I was growing up, I always wanted a cat, but I didn't get one until my tenth birthday. She's a beautiful Russian Blue named Kiki.

That's not the kind of pussy I want to discuss, but I guess I'll take this little piece of information.

> Ty: I take it you don't have her anymore.

> Indie: I mean, she's still around but lives happily with my parents.

> Ty: Hence why you got Bowie?

> Indie: I got him several years later, but yes. Did you have pets while growing up?

> Ty: No. My mother was barely able to keep up with us.

> Indie: How many siblings do you have?

> Ty: A brother and a sister. How about you? Which one of the Decker twins is your father?

I regret the last question though as I recall Jude mentioned her being a very private person who didn't like to talk about their family.

133

Indie: That's classified information. I only feel comfortable releasing such details to my close friends. Though, I want to clarify that they're triplets—Aunt Ainsly is not in show business though.

> Ty: We might not be friends yet, but I'm trusting you with my daughter.

Indie: True.

> Ty: So . . .

Indie: This stays between us. I'm Jacob's daughter and have six siblings. Obviously, you know about Jude. He's the oldest along with his twin, Gabe. Though if you ask them, they'll say Gabe is the oldest. Then we have Harper, Lyric, Lyndon, and Coda.

> Ty: So, you're the baby?

Indie: Nope. I fall between Lyric and Lyndon. Do you get along with your brother and your sister?

I scoff. Me getting along with those two that would be like . . . I don't even know how to describe my relationship with them. Rocky? That's too simple. If I don't see them again that'll be too soon. Abelard and Anastasia are . . . Is there even a word to describe them? I settle for a casual response though.

> Ty: Not really.

> Indie: That long pause means something. It's okay if you don't want to talk about them.

> Ty: Thank you for respecting my privacy.

> Indie: Just treating you how I'd want to be treated. No pressure to share what you're not ready to.

> Ty: So, you have some secrets too, huh?

> Indie: Everyone has secrets.

> Ty: But someone knows yours, right?

> Indie: Nope. It's safer to keep them locked away, right where they belong, in the dark.

> Ty: That sounds awfully whimsical.

> Indie: There's nothing magical about them. It's just . . . I made a few mistakes when I was younger, and I'd rather not disclose them to anyone.

I smirk, nudging back.

> Ty: Let me guess . . . you blew curfew a few times?

Indie: (releases maniacal laugh)

> Ty: Clearly that's not it then.

Indie: Nope. I never had the need to do something like that. The times I wanted to skip school I would ask permission from my parents.

> Ty: That doesn't sound fun or daring.

Indie: My aunt's the principal—and our neighbor. You can see how playing hooky would have been stupid.

> Ty: Then what secrets are you harboring? I can't possibly think of anything a person like you could've done. Underage drinking?

Indie: Leave it, you'll never guess.

I shake my head with a wry smile. The mystery only makes her more intriguing. Still, I can't resist prodding.

> Ty: You can't blame me for trying to uncover the enigma that is Indigo Decker.

Ice, Love, & Other Penalties

> Indie: Nothing enigmatic here, I'm pretty boring! YOU on the other hand . . . You're a puzzle and there's not much about you online.

I freeze, my smile fading. Wherever she's going with this feels like dangerous territory. Still I ask: *How so?*

> Indie: A single dad hockey star—now that's intriguing. No current girlfriend? No word on Myra's mom?

I stiffen. The old defenses rising quickly. That's a question that never comes up in a conversation and my publicist and agent know that it is off-limits. I should call them and ask why they haven't told the Seattle Sasquatches. And since it is clear that Indie isn't aware of that, I say, *Leave it.*

> Indie: (smirks innocently) I see.

I recoil slightly.

> Ty: What does that mean?

> Indie: I seem to have stumbled onto your Achilles' heel.

My jaw tightens. Myra isn't a weakness—her mother on the other hand . . . that situation is complicated. Uncomfortably so. If I can help it, that's something I'll never disclose to anyone. Not even my own child.

After a long pause, Indie texts back, *It's okay. You don't have to go all silent on me. I get it though. There are things that shall remain in the dark.*

I exhale, shoulders loosening. She's right—if her hidden past is half as complex as my own, I understand her need for privacy all too well. Sometimes I wish I could open up about Myra's origins, but experience has taught me caution about whom to trust.

> Ty: Thank you for understanding.

> Indie: Go to sleep. You have a long day ahead of you tomorrow.

> Ty: Talk soon.

I set down my phone, weariness settling over me. As I prep for bed, my thoughts keep drifting back to Indie. Will we ever trust each other enough to share our secrets and more?

Chapter Eighteen

Indigo

THREE WEEKS. It's been three weeks since I started helping Ty with Myra. Tonight, with Myra already tucked in and dreaming, I find myself alone in the living room, gathering scattered toys and remnants of our game night. She likes to play board games and this is maybe the third time I lose track of time and we have to rush to get ready for bed.

I hope this doesn't become a thing, or that Ty notices that I've disrupted Myra's nighttime routine. Not that he can do much to control it, I'm the only person who can look after his child. We still haven't found anyone who meets his criteria or if they do, their background and criminal check doesn't come back clean enough to be caring for a minor.

Though, I seriously need to figure out a way to get out of this assignment. It's not like I spend all my day with Myra—or Ty. I just work for him during game days, and stay overnight when he travels. We've settled into a routine of sorts. Well, I'm actually the one who has a schedule, timing my arrivals and departures to barely overlap with Ty's schedule.

I carefully avoid him so we barely have physical interactions. Though, I've done a poor job when it comes to text. We exchange them so frequently they've become a surprisingly significant part of my day. It's a contradiction I'm still trying to define—or avoid.

As I straighten cushions and fold a forgotten blanket, I can't help but reflect on our situation. Do we even have a situation?

I don't want to find him attractive, but it's almost impossible. It's not that he's not hot—because he is—it's more the way we can easily talk about any subject or he tells me things that I feel are too personal and make him sound vulnerable.

Ty and I, we're like two ships passing in the night, always aware of each other's presence but never quite crossing paths. Except, sometimes it feels like he's becoming my friend.

Our texts started as check-ins about Myra—updates, funny anecdotes, pictures she's drawn that day.

Questions about places to visit or explore during the weekends and where to buy clothes that she might like.

Gradually, those texts are morphing into something unexplainable. I hate to be waiting for them or that sometimes I tell him more than I would to any other friend. We share snippets of our days, jokes, and even pictures of the places we're at. It's strange to think how someone can be so present in your life without actually being there.

I pick up Clara, one of Myra's favorite dolls, and set it in the basket so I can take it upstairs to her room. It's scary to have a routine in someone else's house though. I know I avoid Ty, not out of necessity, but perhaps out of fear. Fear of becoming friends and losing him because he's here for as long as he plays. One day he might go back to Florida or some other place.

And there's that other thing that could happen to me. What if I fall in love with this guy? He's thoughtful and friendly and . . . I should start limiting texts to just check-ins and not . . . Well, getting to know him.

As I turn off the lights and head upstairs to my room, my phone buzzes with a new message. It's Ty. I can't help but smile, despite myself, and open the text.

> Ty: Just arrived at my room, which is too quiet without Myra. How is she?

> Indie: Doing perfectly fine and sound asleep. She beat me at chutes and ladders—twice.

> Ty: Did you two stay up late playing?

> Indie: I don't know what you're talking about.

Ty: You think she doesn't tell me when she goes late to bed.

> Indie: She tattletales on me?

Ty: No, she tries to get away with staying up a little longer—just like she does with Indie.

> Indie: Oh, you haven't said anything.

Ty: It didn't seem important.

> Indie: Okay, I'll tell you all my secrets on how to convince her to do something. How do you get her to bed on time?

Ty: I have an alarm. It's the best and only way to keep track of the nighttime routine. :wink: emoji

> Indie: Okay, I learned something new. I'll set that up so I'm aware that we need to cut the board game time short.

Ty: You should plan on staying for dinner tomorrow so I can beat you at chutes and ladders.

> Indie: Umm, no. I don't want my self-esteem to suffer more than it already has.

Ice, Love, & Other Penalties

Ty: At least I can cook for you.

Indie: You'll arrive tired. I already prepped you a meal, it's in the freezer. You can put it in the oven —I left the instructions on top of the counter. I should be here on Tuesday for your next game.

Ty: Lucky for me, I'll be in town all next week. Is it crazy to say that I miss the drizzle and murky weather?

Indie: You don't, but if you tell yourself that enough it might be true.

Ty: If you move out, will you miss it?

Indie: Out of the state? I've moved out a few times. Every summer we spent it in sunny California or on the road with Dad. I'm not here because of the weather, but my family. Maybe what you miss is Myra and not the gray skies.

Ty: That could be it. So, have you been on tours?

Indie: Ugh, I forget you get all starry-eyed when I bring up my father.

Ty: His music is good.

> Indie: As much as I enjoy discussing my father and his music (not), I have to let you go. Get some sleep and safe travels.

Ty: Thank you, at least tonight I'm sleeping in the same time zone. I'll let you know if I can't pick Myra up from school. You can always drop by any day before Tuesday. You still owe us brunch.

> Indie: Tomorrow is Saturday. Remember I gave you Gabe's address? You're supposed to swing by and get Myra from his house after two.

Ty: Right, you found another way to avoid me.

> Indie: No. Your daughter has a playdate, you're welcome.

Ty: We'll go with your version, but I'm sure I'm right.

Chapter Nineteen

Ty: Your brother Gabe is identical to Jude but . . . they seem so different. How's that possible?

Indie: Twins are two different people—not clones. But ... if you must know, one takes life too seriously, the other one likes to do the opposite of his twin. It's weird, but deep down they're both amazing brothers. So, I take it you picked up Myra from the playdate and now you want gossip? Though I'd love to chat, I'm busy.

Ty: So you say. Your brother said you were just hanging out with your sisters or cousins.

Indie: Girls' weekend is important. So if you have nothing more important to say, let's chat another day.

Ty: I reached out because you never responded to my 'I landed' message. Also, I wanted to discuss your brothers—it was a shock to see how much he looks like Jude. And this might be overstepping, but why does Cora call him Uncle Gabe—I thought he was her father?

Indie: That's something my brother doesn't share so . . .you'll have to forget about that. Your text . . . I sent you a message before telling you that I had dropped Myra at Gabe's. I think that was plenty of communication between us.

Ty: So we're back to one word texts or ignoring me. Got it. So, if Myra wants to invite Cora for a sleepover . . . How do I handle it?

Indie: Tell her Cora isn't allowed to have or go to sleepovers until she turns seven.

Ty: Is that some shit you're making up or a rule?

Indie: A rule—unless it's to her cousin's house, Cora isn't allowed.

Ice, Love, & Other Penalties

> Ty: Should I impose that rule too? At some point Myra will have more friends and what if they invite her to sleep over?

> Indie: I don't know . . . Do you want her to go to someone else's house?

> Ty: I never thought about it until today.

> Indie: Maybe take this slow. She might not be ready either. Start with playdates with friends or . . . I should find you a book. Socializing at a Kindergarten Age.

> Ty: I don't think that's a real title. I would've read it by now.

> Indie: You read parenting books?

> Ty: How do you think she's survived for the past five, almost six years? I didn't have the best example so . . . I had to learn the theory and practice hoping not to fuck her up as much.

> Indie: You're a good dad, Ty. Give yourself a little more credit.

> Ty: I feel like I'm failing.

> Indie: Speaking of she's almost six, what are your plans for her birthday?

Ty: Not sure yet, I still have a month to think about it.

Indie: November 15th is pretty close. If you need help organizing a party, let me know.

Ty: Thank you for the offer. To be honest, we've never celebrated big. We're usually on the road or between games. I usually get her a cake and take pictures.

Indie: Then, we definitely need a party for her. Did your mother ever celebrate her?

Ty: Nope. My mother isn't good at remembering special dates. You're probably right. I'm going to need your help to celebrate her birthday. We can start organizing it next weekend and we can have brunch at your house. You owe us.

Indie: We'll see.

Ty: What about ballet lessons? Myra mentioned something about Cora taking classes and her wanting to do it too.

Indie: I can help you with that and other after-school programs. We can compile a list of activities and places where she can go.

Ty: Cool, I never thought about all that, though I should've. That's exactly how I got into hockey.

Indie: Finally, we're learning more about Mr. Brynes himself. Tell me more.

Ty: That's all you get. I have a little one to attend to and unless you plan on joining us to get our groceries and join us for dinner I'm going to have to leave it at that.

Indie: Talk soon.

Chapter Twenty

Indigo

"Well, this is a surprise," Harper says, pulling the door open.

I brush past her into our childhood home and collapse onto the couch, leaning my head back and squeezing my eyes shut.

What the fuck just happened back there?

"You, okay?" she asks.

Ice, Love, & Other Penalties

I inhale and exhale slowly, trying to avoid passing out because I can't even remember how to breathe. Once I'm sure I remember the process, I nod. "Yeah, just dealing with work stuff." My voice comes out breezy, calm. I'm so fucking chilled no one would think that less than thirty minutes ago I had a very intense encounter with my . . . Is Tyberius my boss?

No, I'm just some stranger giving him a hand while doing a poor job at searching for a permanent nanny. Maybe I should quit the team and find something new to do like . . . What could I do? My parents will remind me that it's time to go back to school. Mom might even say that she has a spot in her PR company for me.

Love the place, I have no trouble doing what she does—I started interning for her when I turned fifteen. But I don't want things to be handed over to me just because I'm her child. I want to work toward it and . . . deserve it.

"Need some tea or warm milk?" Harper asks, her voice reminds me so much of Mom's when she's concerned about us.

I open one eye, sliding her a wry smile. "Why would I want that?"

Harper's dark brown eyes soften with worry as she gazes at me, taking in my tense shoulders and troubled expression. She sits next to me, turning her body toward mine.

"You seem upset," she points out, placing her hand on top of mine. "I'm trying to help with your anxiety, unless you want to discuss what's bothering you."

My throat tightens. There's no way I'm talking about this with her or anyone. Harper's eyes search over my face.

I let out a little huff and shut my eyes again. "There's nothing to talk about. Just thinking about quitting my job."

"The nanny gig or are you finally giving your two weeks' notice to Jude?"

I swallow hard when I think about my brother. Then there's Myra and obviously I can't just leave them like that. That little girl has gone through so much, jumping from one place to another and . . . She's only now adjusting to this new life.

But after what happened earlier . . .

Myra left the show-and-tell bag in her bedroom this morning. The teacher couldn't get ahold of her dad, so they called me since I'm the emergency contact. Since when is show-and-tell an emergency? Why couldn't they just switch her day from Monday to Tuesday or . . . What happened to me is their fault.

Well, it's mine too.

Instead of saying, not my problem, what did I do? I drove immediately to Ty's place and when I arrived, I rushed toward the stairwell and the sight of Tyberius Brynes stopped me in my tracks.

He stood at the landing, shirtless, a towel slung low on his hips, showcasing every inch of his sculpted torso—muscular arms, broad shoulders, rock-hard abs with ridges I wanted to trace with my tongue.

I sucked in a breath. Frozen. My eyes drank him in greedily. That magnificent body I'd been secretly fantasizing about for days was finally bare before me.

As he descended, droplets of water still clung to his skin. I imagined tracing their path with my tongue, tasting every inch of him. The thought made my mouth go dry.

He cocked an eyebrow, his lips curving into a knowing smirk that made my knees weak. "See something you like?"

Heat flooded my cheeks. I crossed my arms tightly, feigning nonchalance. "I'm just here to grab Myra's stuff for show-and-tell. They tried to call you but you didn't answer."

His smirk widened as he reached the last step, bringing him just inches from me. Being this close, his masculine scent enveloped me—sandalwood, spice, pure male temptation. I swayed unsteadily, dizzy with desire.

Get it together, Indie. *I scolded myself.* Actually, get out of here now before you do something reckless.

I took a subtle step back, needing space to think straight. "So, um . . . I'll just head upstairs."

But he moved with me, eliminating that sliver of distance in one smooth stride. His eyes blazed trails over me, hot and hungry. They dropped deliberately to my mouth before rising to meet my startled gaze in a silent question. "Eager to get out of here so fast?"

Before I could respond, he hooked a finger under my chin, tilting my face to his. My lips parted in surprise as his face hovered a breath from mine. "You're so fucking beautiful," he whispered.

I shivered at the desire in his tone, the challenge in his simmering gaze. And I didn't back down. He thinks he's the predator here, but this little lamb has teeth. I devour men like him for breakfast and never look back, *I thought to myself.*

His eyes smoldered. Without another word, his mouth claimed mine in a searing kiss.

His lips were firm yet gentle as they teased mine open. I sighed into him, spearing my fingers through his damp hair to pull that hard body tighter against me. We melded together in a feverish embrace, the towel between us growing maddeningly thin.

Ty kissed me deeply, thoroughly, like a starving man at a

feast. My knees weakened and I clung to broad shoulders, dizzy from his taste.

When we finally broke for air, his eyes seared into mine. "I've wanted this since I first saw you," he admitted roughly.

My lips curved coyly. "What took you so long?"

He chuckled low in his throat, hands framing my face with unexpected tenderness. "I'm trying to be a gentleman here, but you make it damned hard, darling."

"Who said I want a gentleman?" I purred back boldly.

His sharp intake of breath gratified me. I reveled in the power I held over him, that I could make this strong, commanding man come undone with just a touch.

Tyberius grasped my wrist, stilling my movements. His jaw was taut with restraint. "Are you sure you can handle me, Indigo Walker?"

I sighed, taking a step back. "I could, but then you'd lose the only person who can look after your child. I'm stopping for her, because if anything happened between us, you'd never see me again."

Turning around, I headed toward the door. When I opened it, I glanced over my shoulder. "Her show-and-tell bag is on her bed. Take it to school for me, please. I'll see her tomorrow before you head to the game."

Chapter Twenty-One

Indigo

"Hockey guy again, huh?" Harper guesses, jolting me from the vivid memory.

My eyes open wide, alarmed that she might see through me. "What?" I ask pretending not to understand what she's trying to say.

She gives me a knowing look, arching her brow.

"Clearly your stressful work situation involves Mr. Hot Single Dad. Did something happen with you two?"

I nervously brush the tips of my braid, debating where to even begin. Should I tell her? I never talk about the guys I fuck with my sisters. Not that there are many, also, they're just flings and not worth my time. This though . . . Tyberius didn't fuck me, he . . . Why did I let him kiss me?

As I debate how to respond, my traitorous fingers drift lightly to my still-tingling lips, their sensitivity heightened from the bruising kiss Ty imprinted there. I can almost feel the ghost of his mouth against mine—firm yet gentle, hungry and seeking.

Harper tracks the unconscious movement, her eyes widening. "Oh my God . . . did you two kiss?"

"It's complicated," I mutter weakly, fingers falling away from my lips as if scalded. But it's too late—my sister is like a dog with a bone now.

"Well, you have to tell me what exactly happened, because you seem a little unhinged," Harper presses. "Was that kiss good at least? Do you like him? Should I tell our brothers so they can go and kick his fine ass?"

I drag my gaze up to meet Harper's eager one, nostrils flaring with a sharp inhale. Her questions are not helping me one bit. Instead, there's an entire plethora of emotions stirring inside me like a hurricane in the middle of the Atlantic Ocean ready to destroy everything in its path.

Sure, I'm concerned what could happen if the blurred line is erased and we do more than just accidentally devour each other's mouths. There's Myra and Jude to think about, but there's also a lot more.

The way he made me feel when we kissed.

So alive.

As if he knew just exactly how I wanted to be kissed and what I needed from him.

He kissed me, and in that moment, I was reborn. It was as if he'd read the secret map of my desires, charting a course through the unexplored territories of my soul with a precision that left me breathless. I felt seen, known in a way that words could never fully capture.

It was a kiss that spoke of possibilities, of a connection that defied logic and reason.

There's a part of me, reckless and yearning, that wonders what it would mean to forget reason. To explore the depths of this attraction. Of course, I know and that's why I'm terrified of the consequences.

But, oh, how I crave to feel *that* alive again, to be kissed with such understanding, so much need and desire.

And as I grapple with these emotions, these fears and desires, I realize that some lines, once crossed, can never be redrawn.

The damage—well, it can't ever be repaired.

"It was just a stupid moment of weakness," I mutter. "He's hot and it's been a while since I've hooked up."

Harper's eyes narrow, seeing right through my flimsy excuse. Then her expression softens sadly. "Who hurt you, Indie?"

"Huh?" I'm startled by her unexpected question. "I'm telling you I kissed a guy and you . . . What the fuck are you talking about?"

Harper shrugs a shoulder. "I know the signs. Those are pretty obvious trauma responses. Now that I'm healing after—" she pauses, swallowing hard before continuing, "You're pretty evasive about your love life. You make sure that whenever you hook up, you do it with someone you'll never see again. There are several reasons why you keep avoiding intimacy."

I try not to gawk at her little rant. How dare she call me out on something that's none of her business? "There's only *the* one. I'm not interested in relationships," I lash out.

She gives me a sad smile. "I'd believe that from anyone else. But this is you we're talking about."

"You're just trying to look for something that's not there," I say, maybe too defensively.

She presses her lips together, taking a deep breath. "But I see it now. When you came back from New York, we all thought all those panic attacks were somehow separation anxiety. We had babied you a lot—more than we did Coda at the time. He's the baby of the family, sure, but you're our little Indie."

"What does that mean?" I ask.

"You were in the NICU for . . . I can't recall how long. Our parents or grandparents would take us to visit you," she explains to me. "You were so tiny and fragile that it became a thing to protect you. Then, when you were in New York, and then . . . When you came back. None of us wanted to think that something bad could have happened to you. It's easier to believe that you didn't feel safe there because you were away from us," she continues. "But now that I'm going through the same debilitating anxiety, battling night terrors and . . . I'm pretty sure there's something you're hiding from everyone, maybe even yourself."

I clench my fists, pulse kicking as unwanted memories push against their boxes trying to come out. Stay locked where you belong, I order my mind. I don't need any of that to unleash and destroy me again.

"You don't know what you're talking about," I rasp.

She doesn't flinch from my glare. "Actually, I do. I for one feel like an idiot for not doing more when you came back. But it's okay—when you're ready to unload this weight you carry alone, I'm right here. No pressure."

I just stare at her in ringing silence. Because my sister sees too clearly behind my façade, and it terrifies me. The thought of unpacking those memories, those choices I can never take back . . . After all, it was my fault. I shouldn't have been throwing myself at him. But I thought . . . I thought I loved him—and he cared for me.

"You're imagining things." I wave a hand around the house. "It's probably the cabin fever."

Harper scoffs. "It seems like everyone thinks the same. Jude the other day said that maybe I should start getting out because I'm just seeing things. Like him and Bart . . . they have to stop playing around and admit they love each other. Having threesomes with women to pretend they're just having fun is so . . . two decades ago," she states bluntly. "But he says I'm just imagining shit because I don't have a life."

"Oh, but that's not your imagination," I say, knowing that things between Bart and Jude are seriously stupid but they seem to avoid the obvious.

"For sure. Just like now that I'm piecing things together. You're having a pretty bad reaction to Mr. Hockey Guy." She taps her chin. "So, I have a theory, and maybe I'm wrong but . . . I remember you having a huge crush on Frederick. Once you were in college, you mentioned he texted you often. Then you came back, and we never heard about him again."

Panic flutters within me at the direction of her speculation. Does she suspect something about what really happened with Frederick?

I force an indifferent shrug, struggling to keep my voice level. "Yeah, well, girl crushes fade. I grew up and got over it."

But Harper's gaze remains searching, assessing. "Did something happen between you two, Indie? Something bad? Because it seems like he could be the reason, you closed yourself off from relationships."

Schooling my face into careful neutrality, I meet her scrutiny unflinchingly.

"You have an overactive imagination. My romantic history isn't that exciting."

And thankfully, Mom enters the house right as Harper is about to continue badgering me. I feel safe for now, but she's asking one too many questions and I really don't like it.

Chapter Twenty-Two

Ty: I'm sorry if I overstepped.

Ty: Should I be concerned about your silence? I'm truly sorry.

Indie: What are you sorry about?

Ty: Kissing you without permission.

Indie: It was my fault.

Ty: Your fault?

Ty: I'm the one who didn't follow the social cues. When someone comes to my house to pick up something my child forgot I shouldn't be kissing the fuck out of her.

Indie: I should've stopped you.

> Ty: I don't think I gave you enough time for that, which is why I'm apologizing.

Indie: I'm not a victim, okay. I knew what was happening.

> Ty: Somehow, I feel like we're having two different conversations.

Indie: Listen, I'm at my parents. If it's okay with you, let's forget about this.

> Ty: For now.

Chapter Twenty-Three

Indigo

"I DON'T UNDERSTAND why no one wants this job," I drag a hand down my face in exasperation. "We've called so many people and no one is available. Are you sure you don't know anyone who might be available, Mom? You have so many clients who might have worked with a nanny or two."

"The family isn't well versed in nannies. Most of my

clients live in New York or Los Angeles. I doubt they'll be giving up their childcare arrangements for me," Mom replies apologetically.

She's standing by the kitchen counter preparing herself some tea latte.

I'm perched tensely on one of the stools at the large kitchen island, hands wrapped around a mug of hot tea, while Harper sits beside me with her scrutinizing gaze, clearly not ready to let my issues go until she can figure out what's my damage.

Well, she can speculate all she wants. My past remains locked down tight.

Just then Dad enters, Rigby trotting at his heels while he carries Dave's pet carrier. "Did you forget something at my office, Indie?" He gives me a shrewd look that reminds me too much of Harper's probing one. "You left the grandcat and granddog with me, promising to pick them up after you picked up or dropped off something for Myra. Yet, you never came back."

"She was flustered," Harper responds with some satisfaction. She gives me a smug look. "So, he kissed you and you came running to our parents' home. Interesting."

My eyes open wide. She didn't just say that out loud. What is wrong with my sister? We used to cover for each other when we were young. And now . . .

"Who the fuck was kissing you?" Dad frowns deeply. "I don't understand why no one is following my rules."

Before I can deflect, Mom glides over, slipping her arms around Dad's neck to plant a kiss on his scowling lips. "And what ridiculous rule are we talking about now, Jacob."

"Hello, my beautiful twinkle," he mumbles, snaking his free arm around her waist and pulling Mom to him.

"Umm, excuse me. We have impressionable young adults here," I say before this becomes a rated R show. "Can you stop or take this to your bedroom?"

Don't get me wrong, it's amazing to know that my parents still adore each other. However, they should keep their PDA to themselves—go to your room, people.

Mom just laughs while Dad releases her and sets Dave's carrier down, although reluctantly.

I, on the other hand, let Rigby out of the back door. "Don't go too far, boy."

"Woof," he barks and trots away.

Dad clears his throat. "Seriously Indie, are you alright? When you didn't return for them, I almost called your Uncle Mason and had his entire security team search for you."

I press my lips. "Sorry, Dad. Didn't mean to worry you."

His sharp eyes assess me. "No need to apologize, just tell me what happened."

Before I can formulate a response, Mom chimes in. "She's trying to find a nanny for that hockey player."

Dad looks between us. "Let me get this straight, you were going to his house and ended up here frantically trying to line up someone new to watch his kid."

I flush. "I wouldn't call this frantic . . ." But my voice trails off under his scrutinizing gaze, glancing at my notebooks filled with names and laptops pulled up to nanny search sites. Okay, yeah, desperate is written all over this impromptu setup.

Harper grabs Dave's carrier off the counter. "We'll

be in the den. As I told you before, call me when you're ready."

I avert my eyes as she heads out of the kitchen, Mom looking curiously between us. "Is everything alright with you two?"

I nod. "Yeah. Perfectly fine."

"Not really. She's hiding something and doesn't want to confide in me or anyone," Harper responds. "Hence why I'm not very happy with her."

I grimace. "Seriously, Harp?"

"Hey, it's part of my recovery," she claims from somewhere in the house. "I can't keep secrets from those I love. If they ask, I need to respond honestly—no lies."

"So, you know why she's trying to quit this job," Dad presses.

"I already told you. Hockey guy kissed her, and it was so good, she doesn't want to see him again. It has to do with something that happened to her before," she says and then I hear the door shut.

"Bitch," I mutter under my breath.

Dad's blue eyes stare at me. "You want to talk about it? We're here to help you, Indie."

"Sweetie, what happened to you?" Mom's concerned voice makes my chest constrict. I hate it when they worry about me.

"Nothing happened then or now. I'm totally fine," I say, heading out because I don't think I can handle their interrogation. The past is in the past and this stupid kiss is nothing.

I wave. "I'll see you guys later."

"Please don't shut us out," Mom pleads. "Don't do

what Gabe did. Look what happened to him, his silence almost broke him."

"This is nothing like that," I insist walking away.

I make it three steps before Dad calls out, "You forgot the dog, the cat . . . Oh, and your laptop."

I halt in my tracks, cursing internally. After a few seconds of trying to think of what to do I choose the most logical thing. "Have Jude bring them to my place. He owes me."

With that I leave and don't look back.

Chapter Twenty-Four

Ty: Your brother just threatened to smash my face if I ever dare to glance into your direction. Which may become an issue if you're taking care of Myra. Should I wear a blindfold from now on?

> Indie: Oh, God, I swear I'm going to disown my entire family. And that blindfold joke is terrible — don't quit your day job to become a comedian.

Ty: I can be funny when I try, don't kill the dream.

> Indie: What is it you want? I'm not in the mood today.

Ice, Love, & Other Penalties

Ty: So, I take it you told your family about the memorable kiss we shared earlier today. It's good to know that it made an impact on you too.

Indie: First of all, there's nothing memorable about it. It was okay at best. Second, I didn't go telling anyone. My older sister guessed. She told my parents because . . . I still don't understand why this is part of her recovery. It sounded more like a way to fuck with me.

Ty: So, I don't understand who told your brother. Not that I care. I'm not afraid of him.

Indie: Who knows what happened after my sister blurted the information to my parents. We Deckers are like a small town. Gossip spreads like wildfire and it's impossible to extinguish.

Ty: Okay, but let's circle back to the kiss, shall we?

Indie: Forget about it.

Ty: I couldn't even if I tried, but also, you think that kiss was just, okay? We might need to repeat it until I get it right. I was going for something like . . . It was unforgettable, out of this world—best kiss I've ever had.

> Indie: I hate to break it to you buddy, but it wasn't that great. I'd give it a four.

Ty: On the scale of one to three?

> Indie: Ha! Nope. It'd be on the scale of one to twenty.

Ty: Ouch, that hurts. (rubs chest gently)

> Indie: You can't tell me that was an unforgettable kiss. It was just lust and nothing important.

Ty: I see what you're doing.

> Indie: What am I doing?

Ty: You're trying to deny that something happened during that kiss.

> Indie: No. I'm pretty aware that you stuck your tongue inside my mouth. Because that's all that happened between us.

Ty: Call it whatever you want, but you kissed me back, which means you did feel something. If you want to deny it, that's on you.

Ice, Love, & Other Penalties

> Indie: Good sentence, I like the way you started it and ended it. You're not just a jock. Have you thought about writing fictional stories for a living?

> Ty: I'll let your sarcasm slide, because, let's face it, we're talking about something much deeper than a playful kiss here. You're right, I don't just think it—I know it. That kiss? It shattered all expectations, rewrote the rules you've played by. But it's not just about craving another taste, another moment. It's the fear, isn't it? The fear of what it means to need someone so intensely, to have that craving turn into a necessity. You're scared, because deep down, you know. You know that one more kiss, one more moment of surrender, and there's no turning back. You were on the edge of something irreversible, something that could redefine you. And that, my darling, is the real reason you're holding back. The reason why you want me to forget it even happened.

> Indie: That's a pretty arrogant statement.

Ty: I can honestly say that I enjoyed your mouth and I want more—a lot more than just that tiny kiss. I want to burn inside you—have more. That kiss? It was just the beginning. I want the full experience to burn so brightly together that we light up the night sky.

> Indie: Umm . . . that's too intense. It was just a fucking kiss. You do understand nothing can happen between us, right?

Ty: Knowing doesn't put out the fire, does it? It only makes the flames dance higher, more wildly. I'm aware, painfully so, that a kiss isn't enough, but one night is probably all we can have. And here's the thing—I'm not asking for promises. I'm also not offering you forever, or that I'll gift you the moon and the stars. All I can offer is the now, the intensity of a connection that doesn't need to look beyond the horizon of dawn. Your ultimate dream? I can't give that to you. But I can give you a night that feels like a dream, a memory so vivid it'll haunt you, in the best way possible, long after it's over. Just one night, but with the power to eclipse every dream you've ever dared to dream.

> Indie: And according to you, what's my ultimate dream?

Ice, Love, & Other Penalties

Ty: Love. A family.

Indie: Obviously you don't know me. I'm not interested in more from you or anyone. I'm happy with the way things are.

Ty: Huh, that's not what I expected you to say.

Indie: You sound like Harper.

Ty: And she'd be?

Indie: My older sister. She thinks I'm a hopeless romantic who's damaged. She came to that conclusion because I avoid intimacy.

Ty: You avoid intimacy? Yeah, you seem like the kind of girl who'd want a husband, children and a house in the burbs. Discussing your day and your future every night—while cuddling after making love.

Indie: Nope. But it sounds like you're not looking for Mrs. Right either.

Ty: Right for what?

Indie: Getting married, having a family . . . Well, you have Myra, but still, you're not open to love.

Ty: It's a waste of time.

INDIE: SO, SOMEONE BROKE YOUR HEART AND YOU'RE AVOIDING IT, HUH? TELL INDIE WHAT YOUR EX DID TO YOU THAT YOU DON'T BELIEVE IN LOVE ANYMORE.

Ty: My ex didn't do anything.

> Indie: I find it hard to accept your statement. It seems like before you were open to be in a relationship, fall in love. Now . . . Well, you don't. There has to be a good reason why you changed your mind.

Ty: I'm committed to raising my daughter. There's no space for anyone else in my life. And you?

> Indie: I'm too young to think about a serious relationship or love. As I mentioned, I hook up when needed and then it's over.

Ty: No messy feelings? (Glances skeptically)

> Indie: No feelings whatsoever.

Ty: Then, why is it that you don't want to kiss me again? I already promised you that there won't be any messy feelings involved.

> Indie: What if you fall for me?

Ty: I wouldn't, but maybe you're afraid it'll happen to you.

Ice, Love, & Other Penalties

Indie: Ha! You wish.

Ty: There are a lot of things I wish for, and you falling in love with me is not one of them.

Indie: Why are we even discussing this?

Ty: Not sure, but now that I know your expectations, I have a proposition for you.

Indie: What kind of proposition?

Ty: Three letters. FWB

Indie: Fluffy Wombat Buddies? Is that a kink? I like wombats, but I'm not sure if this is for me.

Ty: Good one, but that's not it.

Indie: You want us to become frequent Wandering Backpackers.

Ty: :facepalm: emoji

Indie: Fashionable Wizard Bookworms?

Ty: I'm proposing the ultimate no-strings arrangement. Friends with Benefits. Strictly physical, no emotions allowed.

Ty: Hello, is this thing still on?

Ty: I can see the three dots dancing, either you're trying to figure out a way to let me down or just thinking about the specifics.

Ty: What do you say, darling? We become each other's haven in the night, a sanctuary from the cold, a place where warmth isn't just felt but shared. Then, as the dawn whispers the arrival of a new day, we part, no strings attached, no promises made. It's an adventure, a fleeting journey we take together, knowing full well it ends with the morning light.

> Indie: I don't know . . .

Ty: Consider all the amazing things we can do together—no complications.

> Indie: Can I think about it?

Ty: Just don't draw this out more than we have to, darling.

Chapter Twenty-Five

Tyberius

MYRA GOES TO BED RELUCTANTLY. Not only did she want a bedtime story, but also Rigby to be next to her while I read it.

It's been a month since Indie began to stay with her when I'm away for games, but it seems like it's plenty of time to shift the dynamic of our little family. And where is she when I need her?

Avoiding me because I kissed her senselessly. Not only that, I also told her that we could become fuck buddies. Okay, maybe I pushed her too far. On Tuesday, she sent her sister Lyric, pretending that there's some kind of emergency she had to control. Yesterday, it was Jude who came to watch my child. The general manager missed the game because his sister is avoiding me.

This time the excuse was, she had to go to California to help one of her mom's clients—it was very important. Doubtful. And since she'll stay the weekend there, tomorrow Myra is invited to a sleepover with Cora and her cousin. I wanted to say no but what's the alternative? Miss the game?

Knowing she might not come back, I texted my agent about finding a replacement nanny ASAP. Not really in his job description, but it might be smart to stay away from Indigo Walker before I do something worse—like becoming addicted to her mouth and her body. Or running out of favors and not being able to go to my game.

Though, Byron's response dumbfounded me. He said he was already on it, but what I want isn't available. Apparently, he's friends with the Deckers and Indie reached out to him—clearly also desperate to extract herself from this situation.

So here we are: two desperate people trying to solve the nanny problem because this attraction burns too hot to sustain a professional relationship. Logic dictates that I forget about my proposition, respect her wishes and keep my distance.

But I don't follow fucking logic, only Tyberius rules.

Also I haven't spoken to her in days. So, I grab my phone and text her.

Ty: *I know you said you need time, but how long will it take you to make a decision?*

Indie: *Definitely more than a few days. Why are you messaging me?*

Ty: *Well, I decided to be proactive about my own issue and messaged my agent, Byron Langdon. It seems like you two know each other.*

Indie: *Yep, family friend. He found a couple of people and I interviewed them, they definitely wouldn't work.*

It doesn't sit well that she's adamant to leave the job.

Ty: *So you want to get rid of me.*

Indie: *We kissed, Ty. Things got too intense and I don't want to complicate this.*

The memory of her lips on mine, the feel of her body pressed against me, soft and warm, play on a loop in my mind. Each detail vivid and palpable, as if she were here right now.

I can still taste her, the sweetness of honey that clung to her lips, an addictive flavor that has imprinted itself on me. That kiss was reckless, dangerous, but oh so addicting. Now she wants to leave. The mere thought sends a pang of longing through me, so intense it borders on physical pain.

A longing that shouldn't exist, but I need to satiate. I've never felt this desperate before. Never needed someone like a drug, like air. And I know it's just lust, nothing else. Well no, that's not true. It might also be madness. It's probably the lack of sex.

What if I try to fuck someone tomorrow night after the game? Will this go away?

But I know the answer is no. It's her that I want.

Her mouth, her body, her . . . Everything. Just for one night or as long as she'll have me.

> Ty: Yeah, we definitely had a moment. Great kiss, five out of five stars. Now that you finally admit that there's heat between us, will you accept my proposition?

> Indie: Have I mentioned I don't like to be tangled up with hockey players?

I raise my eyebrows. Has she been with a hockey player before? Or at least in love with one?

> Ty: You never mentioned that before but tell me more. Were you in love with one and he broke your heart?

> Indie: I've never been in love.

> Ty: You don't need to lie to me, darling. This is a judgment-free zone.

> Indie: I'm not lying. Did I have a stupid girl crush? Sure, but I wasn't in love. How about you? Have you been in love?

> Ty: A couple of times. Nothing earth-shattering, no broken hearts. Probably some disappointment, but that's all.

> Indie: You disappointed her?

Ice, Love, & Other Penalties

> Ty: Why would you think I'm the one who did something wrong? Anyway, I just realized you're one of those.

> Indie: One of what?

> Ty: Those people who like to drag information from others, but refuse to give any away.

> Indie: I do like information. Isn't there a saying, information is power?

> Ty: I don't think there is, but you can make it a thing. Now tell me which hockey player broke your heart.

> Indie: No one broke my heart, it was just a stupid childhood-crush.

> Ty: What's his name? Tom, Jack, Peter?

> Indie: It's old history, let it go.

> Ty: If it was, you wouldn't mind telling me his name.

> Indie: His name is Frederick. He was my brother's friend.

It takes me only a second to realize that she might be talking about someone I know. Frederick Rossi was a rookie when I played for the Boston Blizzards. He claimed to be best friends with Jude Decker. He used that name a lot to score women.

And of course, I dare to ask her:

> Ty: Are we talking about Frederick Rossi?

Indie: Leave it alone.

> Ty: Okay, so we're talking about him.

Indie: There are thousands of men named Frederick.

> Ty: But not many were born in Seattle, play hockey, and are close friends with a Decker. He liked to tell everyone about his best friend.

Indie: They were childhood friends. I wouldn't say best.

> Ty: So, I'm right. It was him.

Indie: Don't you have anything else to do tonight?

> Ty: Probably, but all I can think of is you and our deal. You've been great at avoiding me by the way. Sending Lyric, then Jude . . . tomorrow is a sleepover with Cora and her cousin. Ingenious.

Indie: We don't have a deal and I'm busy. Mom needs my help.

Ice, Love, & Other Penalties

> Ty: Just say yes, darling.

> Indie: Good night. I have things to do.

> Ty: Oh, I'll have the best night. I'll be dreaming of your mouth, and the things I'll do to your body once you say yes.

Chapter Twenty-Six

Tyberius

It's just a little past ten o'clock when I pull up to Indigo's place. After dropping Myra off at school, the car almost steers itself in Indigo's direction. Okay, that's a pretty lame excuse, when I had to call Harper to beg her for her sister's address. That sleepover on Saturday was . . . helpful. I got to meet Lyric and Harper in person. Also, I got their phone numbers in case I had an emergency on Sunday.

Of course now that I stand in front of her door, heart thumping in a rhythm that feels too loud in the quiet of the morning, I'm regretting my decisions. I'm nervous with anticipation. Me, Tyberius Brynes who's used to facing down opponents on the ice and play in front of big crowds, I'm fucking nervous.

It's probably because I've never been in this situation. Knocking on the door of a woman who's turned my life around in a matter of weeks—no, days. A few moments pass, stretching out longer than I'd like, and then the door swings open. Indigo stands there.

"Tyberius? What are you doing here?" she asks, her voice laced with a note of annoyance, her eyebrows knitting together in a glare that's meant to be intimidating.

I stare, momentarily caught off guard, not by the unexpectedness of the confrontation but by her beauty. It hits me, as if seeing her for the first time. It's that sharp intake of breath when you're confronted with something so stunning it momentarily disorients you.

The air between us crackles with an intensity that's both exhilarating and terrifying. For a fraction of a second, the world seems to pause and I forget how to speak.

Calm the fuck down, Tyberius. This is just a quick visit to settle things between you two. Take the awkwardness away, not make it worse.

Right, those were my motives.

Pulling my shoulders back, I clear my throat. "I wanted to say thank you. For everything you've been doing for Myra . . . for us. I know I made things awkward, but I want you to know that I really appreciate everything." I hold out the offerings I've brought with me—a small bouquet of flowers, tea from the place Harper mentioned, and an assortment of pastries from the bakery near Myra's school—also Harper's suggestion. Indie's sister is nothing but a fountain of knowledge and she seemed to like me after we had a small chat.

Indigo's eyes widen slightly at the sight, a smile breaking through her annoyed façade. "You didn't have to do this, Ty," she says, but she steps aside to let me inside her home.

"I know I didn't have to. I wanted to," I admit, stepping into her space.

As I enter her house, I'm greeted by an open, airy space where natural light floods in through large, floor-to-ceiling windows, illuminating the eclectic mix of textures and colors. It's like walking into this cool, modern space but with a total bohemian twist. A comfortable, light pink sofa that just pops against the sage green walls. And the walls? They're not boring at all—covered in these colorful, abstract paintings that just make the whole room vibe, just like Indie.

"Though I want to believe you, I think you're here because you want your answer," she states with a serious face.

She then proceeds to take the tea and pastries, setting them on a nearby table, then turns to accept the flowers with a soft, "Thank you."

When our gazes lock, there's an undeniable charge, a surge of electricity that courses through the very air between us. It's a moment so brief yet so intensely charged, it feels as if the world around us falls silent, acknowledging the gravity of our connection.

This isn't just attraction. It's a magnetic pull, as inevitable as the tide drawn to the moon. Our bodies seem to lean closer of their own accord, as if drawn by a force beyond our control. The air between us vibrates with a force I can't fight. Our breaths are about to touch, I'm ready to surrender when she takes a step back.

"Fuck," I mutter under my breath.

"I'm still thinking about your proposition. You can't just barge into my house with my favorite flowers, tea, and even pastries," she says with a firm tone that leaves no room for argument.

"It's just a gesture to erase the awkwardness between us."

She chuckles and shakes her head. "And trying to kiss me was to . . ." Her voice trails, as if expecting a lame excuse.

I shrug. "Sorry, I wish I could make up a lie, but I don't like to start our deal with lies, darling."

"We don't have a deal."

"Just say yes, beautiful."

We stare at each other. the air between us thick with tension.

"Indie, I'm begging you."

She stands motionless, eyes locked on mine. "This is reckless. We shouldn't do anything. In fact, you should fly your mother here or find another way to care for Myra. We need to stop now before things get too complicated."

"They're so simple," I say, disregarding her concerns.

"Why? Why me, Ty?"

Her question is so simple, yet so complicated.

"I want you," I say, my voice low and gravelly. "Your body. Your pleasure. Everything."

I make my desires clear. This isn't about hearts and flowers. There's no romance involved.

This is raw need.

Primal.

An unyielding desire I need to satiate now.

Her eyes flash, a hint of a smile playing on her lips. So beautiful it makes my chest ache.

I step closer, crowding her space. She tips her chin up, gaze unwavering. My fingers trace her jawline, down the slender column of her throat. Her pulse flutters under my touch.

Leaning in, I capture her mouth in a searing kiss. A promise of things to come. She melts against me with a soft moan, her hands fisting in my shirt. Her hands, desperate and seeking, pull me closer, as if she could meld me into her very skin. My hands roam her back, feeling the curve of her spine under my fingertips.

The intensity of our embrace reaches its peak, a moment from which the only way forward is a gentle yet inevitable withdrawal. It is she who pulls away first, her hands against my chest firm yet controlled, conveying much without words. As she steps back, the sudden coolness of air sharply contrasts with the warmth we shared moments ago. Her breaths come quick and shallow.

Her eyes, wide and shining, lock with mine, filled with a mix of emotions—desire, fear, hesitation.

The playful smile that graced her lips just moments before now shifts to a complex look. There's only a breath of separation between us; I bend, resting my forehead on hers. "Tell me yes," I rasp.

She stares at me for what feels like forever until she answers by crushing her lips to mine again. Message received.

Her kiss leaves me reeling, my blood on fire. She arches up, seeking more contact. I oblige, my mouth finding the sensitive spot under her ear. She gasps, tangling her fingers in my hair.

"Ty," she breathes, the sound of my name on her lips nearly undoing me.

My hands trail over her body, learning her curves. She writhes under my touch, soft sounds of pleasure escaping her. I capture them with my mouth, kissing her deeply.

I can't stop, but I know I should before I fuck this up.

Chapter Twenty-Seven

Indigo

Ty's eyes bore into mine, his gaze intense and commanding. I feel my heart race as I struggle to find the words he so desperately wants to hear.

"Tell me yes," he implores again, the rough timbre of his voice weaving a spell that I find increasingly difficult to resist.

Ice, Love, & Other Penalties

I stare at him, unsure of everything.

What am I doing? I dig my teeth into my bottom lip, trying to decide if I'm being stupid or just careless.

He's asking, giving me a chance to say no and push him out of my house, but . . . What if?

I could simply play pretend right now. Pretend this is another life. Pretend that my body isn't humming with desire for this man—just lust because I need sex.

Pretend that he wasn't him, and most of all, I'm not me.

Pretend that I can be whole just for today.

I pull him toward me and kiss him.

And this kiss is completely different from the others. He moves the same way he does everything. He controls us, while demanding I give everything.

He moves us effortlessly to the couch, his grip confident, and suddenly, I find myself sitting across his lap, his warmth enveloping me. He doesn't hold back. He slips his hand under my shirt, groaning as he realizes I'm not wearing anything beneath it. He cups my breasts with both hands. "Fuck, yes," he growls, breaking the kiss. "You have no idea how much I want this. You."

His words send a shiver down my spine, butterflies taking flight in my stomach. I can feel the heat of his palms through the thin fabric of my shirt, and it excites me. I lean into him, my fingers running through his hair as I return his kiss. It's intense, passionate, and it scares me a little.

The intensity of our connection, the raw need that flows between us, it's overwhelming, disarming, and inescapably real.

And as much as it frightens me, it also thrills me, this undeniable pull toward him, toward us. In his arms, I'm not just surviving the moment. I'm living it, fully and irrevocably drawn to the flame of his being.

My entire body trembles with anticipation as he reaches out and takes the hem of my shirt in his big, strong hands. He stares into my eyes, reflecting a hunger that matches my own, as he slowly and seductively pulls my shirt upward, revealing my nakedness to his hungry gaze. I can feel the cool air against my heated skin. Goose bumps erupt all over my body in the best possible way, and I shiver with anticipation.

With a groan that sends shivers down my spine, Ty's lips drop to my collarbone, his warm breath teasing my sensitive skin. His tongue swirls and licks, leaving a trail of fire in its wake, making my knees weak.

He nibbles and kisses his way down my neck, his strong hands exploring every inch of me, as if he were mapping my body with his fingertips, memorizing every curve, every valley.

Finally, his mouth finds my nipple, and his hot, wet tongue flicked across the hardened peak. I moan, arching my back, offering myself to him. His lips close around me, sucking gently at first, then with increasing pressure, teasing and tormenting me until I think I might combust with need.

His teeth graze my aching flesh, sending me over the edge, and I moan his name, my fingers digging into his hair as I clutch him closer.

"Fuck," he groans, his teeth scratching my sensitive skin while his tongue soothes those bites. Heat pools low in my belly as his hands pull down my leggings, exposing me.

I want to do the same, undress him, touch him. He feels so hard and thick under me, I want to ride him. Though, he doesn't let me.

"It's your turn first," he claims. "Be a good girl, and I'll reward you."

His words ignite a fire within me, the smug assurance in his expression challenging, enticing. There's something undeniably provocative about the way he looks at me, a spark in his eyes that says he knows exactly the effect he has on me. And despite the part of me that wants to resist, to push back against his control, I find myself drawn in, caught up in the tantalizing game he's playing.

"But I really want it," I whisper back, defiance laced with desire in my voice. I grind against his cock with deliberation.

I can feel him, hard and thick. The sensation sends a thrill through me, a rush of power and desire. In his eyes, I see not just smugness, but a challenge, an invitation to delve deeper into the depths of our need, to explore the spaces between dominance and surrender.

He looks up at me, green eyes dark with hunger. "Be patient," he growls, dragging his teeth along my neck.

I'm about to expire. Come hard. He masterfully finishes taking off all my clothes and once I'm stripped of everything, he pulls my legs apart.

"You're so fucking wet for me," he says. His fingers trail up my leg, leaving a tingling wake of electricity in their path. He pauses when he reaches my most sensitive spot, his thumb pressing lightly against my clit. The pressure is exquisite, making me arch my back and gasp for more.

"Don't toy with me," I order.

He smirks. "Oh, this isn't toying, it's making sure that you enjoy every second. I want to see you come apart, darling."

"Please," I whisper, not sure what I'm asking for, but certain that I need it.

He chuckles, a low rumble that vibrates against my skin as he leans down to kiss me. "Patience, love," he says, his lips brushing against mine. "We have time."

With that promise hanging in the air between us, he begins to tease me with his fingers. He licks my juices off them, savoring every drop as if it's the sweetest nectar he's ever tasted. I whimper at the sensation, my body responding to his touch with an eagerness that borders on desperation.

"You taste so good," he murmurs, his voice husky and the deep sound of it sending a thrill straight to my core.

As he continues to rub me, his thumb never strays far from my clit, applying just enough pressure to keep me teetering on the edge of orgasm. Every time I think I can't take any more, he changes his rhythm or adds another finger, keeping me guessing and begging for more.

"Please," I whimper again, my nails digging into his shoulders as I try to hang on to some semblance of control. "I need . . . I need . . ."

"You need what?" he asks, his eyes dark with desire as he looks up at me. "Tell me what you want, Indie."

I tremble at his words, my heart racing in anticipation.

"Make the ache go away. Please," I beg.

He lifts me effortlessly, his hands firm beneath my

Ice, Love, & Other Penalties

ass, guiding me toward him. My knees spread wide, either side of his head, as he leans back against the couch. I feel his tongue glide over my folds, wet and hungry, like a predator circling its prey.

I gasp, my hips bucking involuntarily against his face, my body betraying my attempts at control. But without warning, he flips me onto my back, his mouth still devouring me. His eyes lock with mine, intense and unwavering, as if daring me to look away. But I can't, not when his tongue is dancing around my clit, sending electric currents through my veins.

"You like that?" he asks, his tone laced with satisfaction. "You want more?"

I nod feverishly, my breath coming in ragged gasps. He slides two fingers inside me, pumping them in time with his tongue, pushing me closer to the edge. And just when I think I can't take anymore, he pulls back, leaving me aching and desperate for more.

"Beg for it, darling," he growls, his voice raw and primal.

I don't hesitate. "Please," I whimper, my voice hoarse and needy. "Don't stop. I need you to make me come."

His mouth on me is like a drug, an addiction I can't shake off. Before I can say anything, his tongue is already dancing inside me, sending shivers down my spine. I moan, my back arching involuntarily as he explores every inch of my body with his lips and tongue. He groans beneath me, his grip on my hips tightening, urging me to move faster.

My orgasm builds inside me, like a tidal wave gathering strength before it crashes ashore. And just when I think I can't take anymore, he slides two fingers inside me, pumping them in time with his tongue, pushing me closer to the edge.

"Oh, God," I gasp, my voice hoarse and needy. "More . . . Please."

This time he listens. His fingers thrust faster, his mouth devours me at the same pace. The fire within me grows, a slow burn that starts deep in my belly and spreads. My whole body tenses, tightening higher and higher. I can feel his hands on me, warm and rough, as he traces patterns on my skin. He wanted me to let go, to lose control, and suddenly, pure pleasure crashes over me. I scream his name.

My breath is shallow and when I open my eyes he's looking at me intensely. "God, you're so fucking beautiful." His voice is hoarse, raw with need.

Our eyes meet, and for a moment, it's like we're the only two people in the world. Then he's sitting back on the couch, holding me, cradling me as if I'm precious. "Thank you," he whispers against my hair.

"For?" I ask, wanting to return the favor, but unable to move. I'm spent.

"Trusting me. Saying yes. I swear you won't regret this," he promises, letting me lean against his chest.

"I should move. This shouldn't involve cuddling," I say but don't move.

"We're friends, darling. This is the part where you let me hold my friend, care for her because I exhausted her," he states.

"You're not what I expected," I say sleepily, trying to regain my strength and move.

This part of the friendship isn't acceptable. I know

what becoming friends could do to me and I can't afford it.

"Close your eyes, you're safe," he says soothingly, but it's definitely an order.

I try to fight it, but as my eyes close I have only one thought: *don't hurt me.*

Chapter Twenty-Eight

Indigo

A LITTLE LATER I stir awake to find a few unexpected things.

I'm naked, covered with a blanket. Dave's cuddling on top of me while Rigby is on my feet. That shouldn't worry me, but what's different is that Lyric sits on the double chaise across from me, gaze enthralled on her computer. There are two mugs on the coffee table and a glass of water.

Why is my sister here? Where's Ty?

"How long have you been here?" I ask, trying to figure out if what happened earlier was an erotic dream.

A very delicious and erotic dream that left me tired but thoroughly satisfied.

"We've been here for about an hour," Harper says, her voice drifting in from somewhere in the house. Probably my kitchen. "Just as Tyberius was on his way out."

"Have I mentioned that he's hotter than I thought in person?" Lyric remarks bluntly as she sets her laptop on the coffee table. One perfectly sculpted eyebrow arches. "So, you two . . ."

Heat floods my cheeks. I cross my arms defensively. "Nothing happened between us. We just talked."

"So you talked naked, huh?" Lyric laughs and Harper joins her, finally stepping into the living room.

I scowl even as my traitorous mind conjures what happened earlier with Ty. "Just leave it, okay?"

Harper picks up a paper that's on the coffee table, next to a glass of water and the bottle of pain meds.

"Thank you for that orgasm, darling. I'll text you later tonight, T." Harper reads with a deep voice trying to imitate Ty's.

"He did not leave that note," I say, wrapping myself in the blanket and standing up.

Harper scoffs, handing it to me. "No, it was even more . . . sweet?"

When I read it, my body flushes all over again.

Thank you for giving me such an extraordinary gift and letting me watch you fall apart, darling. You're gorgeous when you let your guard down. I can't wait to taste you again—all of you.

T.

"So, nothing happened, huh?" Lyric gives me a teasing look, one eyebrow raised in disbelief.

The room suddenly feels ten degrees warmer, and it's not just from the blanket wrapped around me. I clutch the note a little tighter, the words blurring as a rush of embarrassment mixed with something akin to excitement floods through me.

"I . . . It's not what you think," I stammer, my defense crumbling under their amused gazes.

Harper and Lyric exchange a look, a silent conversation that I'm not privy to, but one that clearly involves making me squirm.

"Come on, spill it. Since when do you keep secrets from us?" Harper prods, settling down on the couch with a smirk that says she's enjoying this far too much. But then her face becomes serious. "Oh, right, you've been hiding a lot from your sisters. So much."

Lyric nods. "Are you going to tell us what's going on?"

I let out a sigh, realizing there's no escaping this interrogation. I'm not sure what I should tell them, but take the easiest route. "He offered me a deal, I took it. It's pretty simple. Don't make this into . . . Well, it's really nothing."

Harper crosses her arms, leaning back on her seat. "Really, simple. There's a deal and that sounds like bullshit."

"Bull. Shit," Lyric agrees.

The room is quiet for a moment, the earlier

amusement giving way to a more thoughtful atmosphere. Harper's expression is contemplative. "He called me earlier to ask for your address. Apparently, he called a lot of Deckers to figure out a way to get to you."

I scoff, "You gave him my address?"

She shrugs. "You left a lot unsaid and then disappeared to California. He wanted to smooth things between you two—for his child."

"Did you tell him about the tea, the flowers, and the pastries?" I say a little too harshly, it's hard to contain my anger.

He used my sister to get to me.

"The guy is good. We got to talk and asked me what you liked most, disliked and . . . I didn't give him any hints if that's what you're asking," she states. "It was more like he really wanted to get to you—smooth things over."

Lyric narrows her eyes. "Something about this isn't sitting well—what is it, Indie?"

I shake my head. I hate feeling used and . . . He fucking used me, and I let him.

"Listen, I don't know what's going on between you two, but he really seems to care for you," Harper states. "When we arrived, he asked us not to wake you up. He was concerned for you."

"What deal did you make?" Lyric asks.

I shrug, beginning to walk toward the stairs.

"Talk to us," Harper calls out. "We can't be there for you if you close yourself up."

"Friends with benefits," I say without turning around to see them. "It's stupid. I . . . need to get a real job."

"That's why we're here," Lyric says. "Get dressed so we can talk about my proposition."

When I arrive at my room, I take a quick shower, put on a sun dress and brush my hair pulling it into a ponytail. I pick up my phone from its cradle and realize there's a message from Ty.

> Ty: Sorry to leave before you woke up, but I needed to pick Myra up from school. Also, I couldn't go back to tell you because your sisters were about to disrupt your nap.

> Indie: I really don't know how to react to your note or what happened between us.

> Ty: If I made you uncomfortable let me know. I want this to be perfect for you—as it is for me.

> Indie: I'm trying not to overthink it or feel used.

> Ty: This is just like any other hookup you've had.

> Indie: That's the thing. I'm usually in charge. My rules and my . . . I'm the one who leaves.

> Ty: Oh, you didn't like the dynamic. We should've talked about that. Next time I'll consult with you beforehand. Sorry if this wasn't good for you.

> Indie: It was . . . different. Maybe you're right and we need to set up some ground rules.

> Ty: Okay, next time I go down on you, I'll wait for you to guide me on when and how . . . just don't expect to come fast. I'll still be in charge of your orgasms, darling.

I squirm when I read his text, heat rising in my cheeks. My heart flutters at his words, a wave of desire and nervousness twisting in my stomach. My fingers curl into fists, nails digging into my palms. Do I want this? To give him such control, to cede the reins of my pleasure to him?

Yes. The word whispers through me, sending a shiver down my spine.

I stare at the text, reading it again and again, imagining the scrape of his stubble against my thighs, the warmth of his breath and the slide of his tongue. My breaths come faster, shallow and wanting. I want to give myself to him completely, let him take control of my pleasure and push me past my limits. The thought sends a spike of arousal through me, and I have to bite back a moan.

My phone buzzes with another text.

> Ty: Thinking of you and how wet you'll be for me. I can't wait to taste you, feel you come around my tongue. You were so responsive, so eager to please. My perfect good girl.

I flush, equal parts embarrassment and need. He's

not even here and already I feel boneless and pliant, ready to do whatever Ty desires.

Which is exactly how he wants me.

As I'm about to text back, Lyric calls me, "Indie, we don't have all day. Can you please come down soon?"

I toss my phone back to the bed. Ty teased me and made me wait to get my reward. Maybe I should do the same with him.

Chapter Twenty-Nine

Indigo

When I step back into the living room, the flowers are artfully arranged in a vase, the box of pastries sits invitingly open, and a cup of tea emits a welcoming steam just for me.

"Who told you that you can eat my pastries?" I halfheartedly complain, settling into the couch with a mock frown.

Harper just rolls her eyes, while Lyric chimes in with unexpected news, "We've decided to start a company."

"Just like that?" I'm genuinely surprised, not just by the announcement but by the inclusion. "And why are you telling me this?"

Lyric corrects with a smile, "Oh, I said 'we.' As in you, Harper, and me."

"We are?" The idea seems far-fetched, almost ridiculous.

Harper exhales a heavy sigh, "Don't get me started. I've already tried to tell her I'm broke and a little too broken to be a part of her plan."

"You'll get your money soon—and your patents," Lyric reassures with a dismissive wave of her hand. "Your lawyer isn't just hot, but also pretty good at what he does."

Harper's response is a dismissive eye roll. "Great, so even if I get my patents back, why on earth do you want us to start a company?"

Lyric's eyes light up with enthusiasm. "I love designing clothes, but imagine coupling that with a cosmetics line that carries our brand. It won't be just about the products. It'll about the statement."

I can't help but cut in before she spirals into a full-blown pitch. "While I think it's a brilliant idea, I'm puzzled why I'm part of this equation. You've got the science whiz, and you're the creative genius. I'm . . . Well, I'm just me."

"You're the face of our operation. Our CEO," Lyric declares confidently, as if it's the most natural decision in the world.

"I don't even have a degree," I protest, feeling out of my depth yet intrigued by the boldness of her vision.

"Education isn't the only measure of capability. You have the charm, a way with people, and an authenticity we need at the wheel."

I gawk at Lyric then glance at Harper as if saying, *Are you listening to our sister? She has lost her shit.* But of course, I don't say that. I go for something less daunting, "Can you even do this?"

Admittedly, that came out harsher than intended.

Harper's brow furrows. "What's that supposed to mean?"

"You mentioned a non-compete clause last time you talked about work. You said it bars you from entering the industry for five years," I point out, recalling the injustice of it all. Her ex didn't just hurt her personally and emotionally. He destroyed her professional life too.

Lyric waves away my concern with a confidence that borders on audacity. "As I said, her lawyer kicks ass and more. He's already taking care of the employment issue—including opening her own company. We have plenty of time to plan everything."

"I'm already committed to helping Jude with the Sasquatches," I counter, trying to ground this conversation in my reality. "And then there's Ty . . ."

"Your fuck buddy?" Lyric interjects, her bluntness making me wince.

"I prefer to call him a friend with benefits," I clarify, aiming for a touch of . . . I mean what? She's right. We're nothing more than fuck buddies.

"Look"—Lyric leans in, her voice softer but no less determined—"we're just laying the groundwork right now. If it eases your mind, go ahead and enroll in some business courses. By the time we're ready to launch, your hockey player will have sorted out his childcare situation."

"Can I think about it?" I ask.

Lyric nods decisively. "Alright, that settles it. Indie, your task is to scout for investors, but steer clear of the Deckers. Our family is great, but this venture should be just us sisters."

"I like that," Harper says. "Us against the world, like when we were young."

"Only this time, let's not keep secrets from each other," Lyric adds, her gaze shifting between us. "We're aware of what you've been dealing with, Harper. Now, it's time for Indie to share with the group."

"There's nothing to share," I assert, then—with a pointed look at Harper—add, "She's fabricating things."

"I told you she wouldn't be ready to open up," Harper states. "Not everyone processes things by talking about them and moving on."

Harper's words give me an opening, and I take it. "What about you, Lyric? You've been back from Paris for months. Weren't you supposed to be designing for some kick-ass brand?"

Harper chuckles.

Lyric's response is a soft chuckle, tinged with a hint of bitterness. "I left the internship the second my boss attempted to claim my personal designs as his own." She pauses, a grimace flickering across her face. "I was searching for a new designer house when Pipe and Grace convinced me to come back home."

At the mention of our cousins, Harper stiffens. It was them who found out that our sister had bruises on her arms. Lyr came back so we could be there for Harp while she left the abuser. To stand with her and go from victim to survivor.

"It's hard to admit that the person who loves you is hurting you intentionally," Harper says. "In the beginning, he would apologize. Then, he would blame me for having to do it. It was my fault he cracked a rib or broke my arm. He gaslit me claiming to be the victim."

Lyric and I stand from our seats and hug her.

"I get it, you blame yourself for whatever happened to you, Indie," she continues. "But know that it wasn't your fault, whatever happened. And we're here whenever you're ready to share. If anything, go to a therapist."

"It's on my calendar. I attend weekly sessions," I say, but my voice comes out empty.

We discuss my anxiety, what provokes it and how to cope. He doesn't know about Frederick. No one does. What will I win by saying anything out loud?

I'm sure everyone will think I was an idiot. It's not like Freddie was some stranger who forced himself. We were friends and . . . I just—I feel so ashamed about that night and everything that led to it.

Will this ever get any better?

Chapter Thirty

Tyberius

RESTLESS, sitting in my dimly lit bedroom, my mind recounts my time spent with Indie. Every detail from the moment she kissed me is on replay.

The sensation of her skin against mine. My mouth on her pussy. Her taste, the catch in her breath, the depth in her eyes revealing a whirlwind of emotions—it all lingers with me, tangible and haunting.

Ice, Love, & Other Penalties

I fucking need her.

It's a truth that digs deep, an ache that's both sweet and agonizing.

Compelled by a craving too potent to ignore, my hand moves almost of its own volition, reaching for my phone. In this moment, bridging the gap between us feels urgent, necessary. Given the casual nature of our relationship, friends who happened to share a few benefits, I opt for a bold approach—a sext.

> Ty: I just laid in bed for the last hour thinking about you, guess what I was doing? :eggplant: emoji

As I wait for her reply, my cock hardens. Ah, the thrill of teasing her, of drawing out that blush I can't see but can vividly imagine.

> Indie: :raised-eyebrow: emoji
> Umm what's happening here? Are we supposed to throw vegetables at each other? :red-apple: emoji

> Ty: I'm trying to get back to our earlier text/conversation. Before you left me hanging, darling. I was about to tell you how good you taste—how wet I want you.

> Indie: I recall the conversation.

> Ty: Why did you stop it?

> Indie: My sisters were in the living room. I couldn't continue such a discussion when I was practically shaking and wanting to touch myself while you told me the things you wanted to do to me.

I swallow. Okay, she's good at this. Is she, or maybe she's too honest and is telling me just what was happening—no role-playing. Either way, I want to continue, see how far we can get. But now, I'm curious about her preferences.

> Ty: So I take it you don't like sex in public places.

> Indie: I . . . I wouldn't use the word dislike. Plus, my house isn't a public place.

> Ty: But there were people around who could hear your moan loudly as you touched your pretty pussy. Sliding your fingers in and out imagining it was me.

> Indie: I wouldn't care if they had been strangers. We're talking about my sisters. They'd tease the fuck out of me for eternity. Plus, it'd be embarrassing.

> Ty: So it'd be okay if they were strangers? We could go to a restaurant, and I'll finger you under the table?

I press send before I even checked if I worded it

correctly. But hopefully, she gets the idea and we can get this rolling. I need some relief.

> Indie: Do you use public places to hook up?

I groan, this isn't where I wanted to take this conversation. Come on, darling, be a little less practical and let your desire drive you. Not your curiosity.

> Indie: Oh, you went quiet. So, you go to a bar and fuck the first woman who glances at you.

> Ty: Whoa, that's not the direction I expected us to take. Let's start with no. I don't hook up much, when I do, I'm usually on the road and pay for another room.

> Indie: So, you can leave without saying a word.

> Ty: Is this a trick question?

> Indie: No. I'm curious.

> Ty: If I left today it was because you were sleeping and I needed to pick up Myra. May I remind you I left a note.

> Indie: A pretty embarrassing note my sisters read.

> Ty: My apologies. If I had known they were going to be there I would've hidden the note.

> Ty: Actually, I would've woken you up so you could've dressed up before they entered.

Indie: So, what happens when you're not on the road? How do you hook up?

> Ty: I don't hook up.

Indie: I don't believe you.

> Ty: I have a five-year-old at home. Nothing will happen within the two-hundred-mile radius of the house for the next thirteen years, give or take.

Indie: Yet, here you are telling me you were thinking about me and wanting to fuck around. How does that work?

> Ty: You and I are different, darling. We're friends who'll find time to benefit from each other. Also, this text started as a teasing that I wanted to evolve to role-playing, darling. You were supposed to guess what I was doing, then I would ask if you're wet.

Ice, Love, & Other Penalties

Indie: Ooh, so I would say you were touching a hard thick cock while thinking about me. Then you'd order me to tell you if I'm wet, I'd say I'm soaking just for you. I could even send a voice memo with a moan. But . . . I can't because I'm at my brother's house.

Ty: Which brother?

Indie: Does it matter?

Ty: Probably not, I'm just curious.

Indie: Why do you always want to know everything?

Ty: No, that's you. I'm just wondering if you're at Gabe's since he lives close by and if that's the case, I would ask you to swing by and spend the night with me.

Indie: It's not only me, you also want to know everything, but let's not digress. I refuse to tell you where I'm at.

Ty: So it's Gabe's and you don't want me to beg you to come to me, huh?

Indie: Even if you ask me, I wouldn't go. Remember the five-year-old sleeping a few rooms away from you?

Ty: Well, let me get you a car to take you home. I don't like knowing that you're driving late at night.

Indie: You are . . .

Ty: Don't leave me hanging.

Indie: If you were a few years younger and I wasn't jaded . . . Good night, Ty. I'm turning this off. Let's not talk again until it's time to exchange Myra.

Ty: You make it sound like a custody agreement.

Indie: It's not exactly like that but I suppose that's how we'll handle this. Bye.

Chapter Thirty-One

Indigo

So much for keeping my distance from Ty—at least until tomorrow, or better yet, forever, if I could convince one of my sisters to watch Myra until I find a suitable nanny.

"What now, Tyberius?" I sigh, conflicted by so many emotions swirling within me as I open the front door.

Ty's apologetic smile greets me. He holds out a

paper cup, the aroma of lavender and chamomile tea filling the air between us. "Here's some tea, beautiful. I came by hoping you had time to help me with Myra's party." His words are hesitant, almost shy.

I face-palm mentally, a wave of regret washing over me. "I forgot," I admit, though it's more like I hadn't let myself think much about him or Myra with everything else going on between Ty and me.

Ty's face falls, worry creasing his handsome features. "I didn't exactly forget, but time has just slipped away, and here we are, two weeks away with nothing planned." He runs a hand through his dark hair, frustration evident in his tense shoulders.

I slide my phone from my back pocket, fingers flying over the screen to access his calendar. "The fifteenth is a Friday, and you have a game. Which means . . ." I trail off, calculations running through my mind. "We need to organize the party on the sixteenth. We can get her balloons and special cupcakes for the morning of her birthday—maybe ask the teacher if she can bring a special treat to class."

I look up to find Ty staring at me helplessly, eyes wide. He drags both hands down his face with a groan. "That's a lot of information." His shoulders slump in defeat. "As I said, we never celebrated that much and I've never done that much in so little time. Do you think it's doable?"

"Of course," I reply confidently, smiling in what I hope is a reassuring way. Reaching out, I squeeze his forearm gently. A spark of awareness zings up my arm at the contact and I drop my hand quickly, pulse racing.

Ty blinks in surprise, a slight catch in his breath,

Ice, Love, & Other Penalties

before visibly collecting himself. "And what about the party itself?"

I tap my chin thoughtfully, ideas spinning through my mind. "We could do it in your backyard, invite a few of her friends. Make it a unicorn-themed party, or . . ." I trail off. "My sisters and I can brainstorm something after a trip to the party store. Though, Teddy can get all of that done and more in a day—at a price, of course."

"Anything for Myra," Ty says. "This is her first big party and I want it to be memorable."

"Then it will be," I assure him. "Let's go to my kitchen. We can start up my laptop and figure out what themes there are. Then, we'll call my cousin."

Just as we're about to move, his phone rings loudly. Ty lets out a long, frustrated groan, scrubbing a hand over his face.

I raise my eyebrows curiously. "Who is it?"

"My mother," he spits through gritted teeth, shoulders tensing. He glares at the phone display as if it has personally offended him. "She's been calling all morning, and honestly, I don't have time for her drama right now." His jaw tenses, frustration etched in the strained lines around his mouth.

"And we don't want her to call because . . .?"

He shakes his head, a muscle twitching in his cheek. "Leave it, okay."

I lift one shoulder in a slight shrug. "Sure, but if you need someone to talk to, I'm here." I offer him a small, supportive smile.

"So we're back to being friends," he says, voice dipping an octave lower, a hint of suggestion in his warm green eyes.

I scoff softly, cheeks heating as I break his gaze.

Honestly, I don't know how to respond to his flirtatious words. My pulse skips and stutters, conflicting emotions rising within me.

He takes a step closer, the clean scent of his skin wrapping around me. "We had an agreement and suddenly you shut me down," he states, watching me intently. "What was that about?"

I wet my lips nervously. "Things got too . . . Too intense, too fast," I respond weakly and then immediately regret the admission.

Ty narrows his eyes, searching my face. "Is that so? And you couldn't tell your friend?" His words hold a note of gentle chastisement. "I could've dialed things down. If this is going to work, darling, you have to communicate."

I drop my gaze, shame and anxiety swirling sickly inside me. But that's the thing—I don't know if I want this to work. I can't bring myself to say the words aloud, fearful he'll see me as just a stupid, fickle child. I suck my lower lip between my teeth, heart pounding as I feel myself regressing emotionally.

My breath comes shorter, a vise squeezing my chest. I struggle to control the panicky gasps threatening to burst free, not wanting to completely lose it in front of Ty. But I can feel my rigid composure cracking, fears and doubts assailing me.

Sensing my distress, Rigby pads over and nudges my hand with his cold, wet nose. I cling to his fur like a lifeline as Ty waits patiently for my response. But still my lungs constrict, black spots dancing at the edges of my vision.

Dimly, I'm aware of Ty's concerned face hovering near mine as he says my name. Mortification wars with bone-deep anxiety inside me—I'm falling apart right in front of him over nothing. The thought makes me lightheaded with embarrassment even as I continue to silently fall to pieces.

"Hey, hey, look at me," Ty says gently. He grasps my shoulders, ducking his head to meet my lowered gaze. "You're okay. Just breathe with me, nice and slow."

I shake my head jerkily, gulping air in panicked gasps. But Ty begins taking exaggerated slow breaths, keeping our eyes locked.

"In . . . and out. That's it, just like that," he coaches. His strong hands rub comforting circles on my arms. "You've got this. Just breathe."

Rigby leans more heavily against my legs and I focus on synchronizing my frantic respiration to Ty and my dog's steady pace. Gradually, the crushing weight in my chest eases. My head clears, leaving me exhausted and emotionally drained, but breathing normally.

Ty's eyes crease with concern, his thumb grazing my cheek soothingly. "Better now?"

I give a small, embarrassed nod. But I don't pull away, still leaning on him not only for the physical touch but also for emotional support, which I shouldn't be doing.

Once I'm okay, he glances at Rigby and then at me. "He's a therapeutic pet, isn't he?"

I bob my head a couple of times. Ashamed that someone knows that I can't keep my shit together. That . . . I close my eyes briefly trying to find my strength somewhere within me but it's gone. I feel defeated and I don't even know why.

Ty caresses my cheek with infinite tenderness. "Darling, you're safe with me. I hope you know that. If I had known, I wouldn't have . . ." His voice trails off regretfully.

"I'm okay," I rasp desperately, though I'm anything but. "This doesn't happen often, it's just when I . . . I can't handle intimacy, okay? So, you might as well leave. Me and my sisters will take turns with Myra and Teddy will figure out the party." Mortification makes my words blunt.

He nods a couple of times. "I see. So, when people figure out your weakness you shut them down and it's game over. That would work for many, but we're friends and I'm not leaving you like this."

I inhale a shuddering breath as frustration wars with vulnerability inside me. "You almost said it, you wouldn't have trusted me with Myra if you had known," I accuse unevenly, the words tumbling out laced with hurt. Anger and bitter disappointment in myself churns sickly within. I dig my nails into my palms, fighting back hopeless tears.

Ty doesn't flinch at my outburst. Instead, he catches a lone tear trailing down my cheek with infinite tenderness, the caress undoing me. Wordlessly, he pulls me against his solid chest, enveloping me in his arms. "No, I wasn't talking about Myra," he murmurs into my hair. "But because of what happened between us."

And of course he regrets it. This is exactly why I hook up on my own terms because then no one will be able to reject me, but here I am, being rejected while he's feeling sorry for me. That's the worst combination.

His lips graze my cheek in the softest kiss. "Who hurt you, Indie?"

Chapter Thirty-Two

Indigo

His question resonates inside my head. *Who hurt you, Indie?*

Myself. I don't want to admit it, but I did it and now . . . I do what my parents taught me, live with the consequences of my actions. It'd be too easy to blame Frederick, but it was me who insisted, who wanted him to love me.

"No one," I claim, anger at my weakness bubbling up inside me. I try half-heartedly to push him away but I'm not strong enough, though not because he's forcing the contact. I want to remain here where I feel somehow safe in his embrace.

Ty gently lifts my chin until our gazes lock, his green eyes intense upon mine. "You can talk to me," he coaxes.

Just then his phone blares loudly from his pocket, shattering the moment. He grimaces, arms tightening around me briefly and reluctantly he withdraws from me to check the caller ID.

"It's my mother again," he sighs, tension creeping back into his body. He looks down at me with uncertainty.

"It could be an emergency," I suggest.

He scoffs, jaw clenching. "Everything is life or death with her—but only when it's convenient for her selfish drama." His eyes flash angrily.

I tilt my head, hesitant curiosity getting the best of me. "Why don't you get along with her?"

Ty drags a hand through his dark hair in agitation. "Because she's a shitty, toxic person and an even worse mother," he harshly bit out.

I blink in surprise at his vehemence. Myra seems to love her, I don't understand why they have opposite reactions about this woman. "Aren't you exaggerating a little?"

Before he can respond, the phone screams again. With a humorless smirk on his lips, Ty offers it to me. "Wanna see just how shitty she is?" His tone drips with bitter challenge.

I slide my finger across the screen and set the call on speaker with no small amount of trepidation. "Hello?"

"Why the hell are you answering my son's phone?" a harsh female voice demands angrily. "Are you his new mistress? You slut. Let me guess—you want money, right? Well, I've got news for you, that bastard won't give you anything. He has me rotting in this hellhole nursing home like yesterday's trash while he plays pro-athlete." She breaks off with a spiteful laugh that has me cringing.

I stare at the phone and then at him. He gives me a look that says, 'and that's just the beginning, darling.'

I stare wide-eyed at the phone, shocked by her venom, then back at Ty. His knowing glower clearly says this is mild for dear old mom. I clear my throat. "How can I help you, Mrs. Brynes?"

"Brynes? You think I have the last name of the asshole who knocked me up and left me with a bastard who doesn't give two shits about his mother?" She barks another caustic laugh. "Listen, honey, just tell my useless failure of a son that his mother Lucille called. It's important he knows: Anastasia is clean and wants her daughter back—of course, he'll have to pay us child support. We're not made out of money. Maybe buy us a house in Boca or the Keys. Can you be a doll and give him the message?"

Before I can respond, Lucille abruptly ends the call.

Ty drags a weary hand down his face, tension radiating from his broad shoulders. "And that, in a nutshell, is my toxic mother," he says bitterly.

I'm reeling, confused and conflicted. I have so many questions swirling chaotically in my mind but I hesitantly dare to ask, "Who is Anastasia?" Maybe his mother has a bizarrely close relationship with his ex and that would explain . . . things. I try not to let my rioting emotions show, attempting to keep my expression neutral.

"My half-sister. Same crazy mother, different deadbeat father," Ty replies flatly.

He gives me a quick recount. He's the oldest of three. The brother between him and Anastasia has a rich dad who took his kid when he dropped Lucille. His little sister was born when he was thirteen and though he helped take care of her for five years, once he was in college he left for good—but his mother kept finding him.

I swallow hard, anxiety rising. "So . . . your sister. . . she's Myra's mom?" I force the words out through a constricted throat, working hard to keep my voice steady. Don't freak out, I order myself. And fail miserably.

Ty presses his lips together and gives a short nod. "Yep. She dumped the baby with Lucille soon after giving birth. I never even knew who the father was." His hands curl into fists.

I stare at him, mind reeling. "Myra is your niece?" I finally choke out.

He nods. "Yeah. The moment Lucille realized what was going on, she called me. Said I had to take responsibility since it was 'my blood.'" His mouth twists bitterly over the words. "I couldn't just abandon Myra to the chaos I grew up in. So I adopted her, made her legally mine with my agent's help. None of Myra's history is public knowledge."

"That's why no one knows about her mother," I mumble.

Ty nods, a muscle tics along his tight jawline. "And Lucille uses it against me, leverage to try and bleed me for money." Disgust laces his tone.

"Have you told her?" I ask him.

"To stop harassing me?" He chuckles. "Multiple times, but Lucille doesn't know the word no."

I shake my head. "No. I meant Myra. Have you told her she's adopted?"

Ty scrubs a hand over his face, looking suddenly frightened. "Of course not. I don't . . . You know all the things that could happen if I do?" His shoulders hunch defensively.

I lift one shoulder in a slight shrug. "Probably nothing, if you handle it the right way."

He scoffs derisively. "You have no idea."

I fold my arms across my chest. "My parents told me the truth about my adoption from the very beginning. I've always known that they chose me."

Ty's gaze sharpens on mine in surprise. "I didn't . . . You're adopted?"

I chuckle softly. "Isn't it obvious?" I sweep a hand down my petite frame. "My brothers and sisters are all Amazonian. I'm the only shorty Decker—even Lyndon is tall."

Ty just stares at me, clearly thrown. "Why wouldn't Lyndon be tall?"

"He's adopted too."

"And he knows too?" Ty asks incredulously.

"Yep," I confirm matter-of-factly. "It was never a big deal in my family."

Ty rakes both hands through his already disheveled

hair, exhaling harshly. "If I tell Myra . . ." Fear shadows his eyes again.

"You don't need to do it right this minute," I rush to reassure him. "Maybe start with speaking to a child therapist. Get guidance on the best way to approach it."

He bobs his head a couple of times. "So you know my secret, what's yours?"

Chapter Thirty-Three

Tyberius

INDIE'S GAZE skitters away from mine, something vulnerable and haunted shadowing her delicate features. She looks almost like a startled doe poised for flight. "I don't—"

"Don't bullshit me, darling," I interrupt, though keeping my tone gentle. "I witnessed a pretty major panic attack back there. You completely lost it because I triggered something."

"Me . . . I . . ." She swallows hard. "I had a bad . . ."

"Experience?" I prompt softly when she trails off.

Indie shakes her head jerkily, brown waves tumbling over her shoulders. "I can't even call it a breakup. There was this older guy I thought I . . . loved." She hugs her slim arms around herself in a protective gesture. "Remember I told you how my parents were high school sweethearts?"

I tip my head curiously. "What does that have to do with—"

"I thought I had that with him, you know?" Indie plunges on raggedly. "He paid attention to me and I was just so stupidly in love I didn't realize he didn't actually give two fucks about me." Her voice drips bitterness and shame.

She doesn't look at me when she tells me about this guy, and how excited she was when he finally paid attention to her. An inexperienced teenager who had been longing after him. I don't move when she tells me about the night he visited her in New York. The intensity of the first exciting kiss and how it built into a disastrous moment . . . her saying no, her pleas for him to stop and how he left, disregarding her feelings.

Now I'm the one trying to breathe normally. My hands clench into tight fists as the implication of her fragmented words sinks in. Red haze clouds my vision, fury boiling hotly in my veins at what was done to her.

"If I hadn't—" Indie whispers, a single tear slipping down her pale cheek.

"Indie, none of that was your fault," I interrupt gently but firmly.

She shakes her head jerkily, self-recrimination twisting her delicate features. "For years I threw myself at him. I should've known better."

I grasp her slender shoulders, ducking my head to catch her lowered gaze. "You said no and asked him to stop. That's the only thing that matters." My voice brooks no argument.

"But—"

"You don't want to see yourself as a victim here. I understand that." I choose each word carefully. "But what he did wasn't okay. You did nothing wrong."

Indie presses her trembling lips together. "I just don't want to feel so broken again. But sometimes everything comes flooding back anyway." Her whispered confession twists like a knife in my chest.

My alarm beeps then, reminding me I need to pick up Myra soon. I glance reluctantly down at my watch, then back up at Indie. If I walk away now, she might shut down completely or spiral into another panic attack alone. The thought makes my decision easy.

"You're coming with me," I say decisively.

Indie avoids my gaze, arms wrapped protectively around her middle. "I have things to do." Her tone is dull.

I rake a hand roughly through my hair. "You shouldn't be alone right now. Come with me, just for a bit."

Her delicate jaw firms stubbornly even as she appears to draw inward emotionally. "I'm perfectly fine," she insists through gritted teeth. "I'm an independent woman who doesn't need a man to dictate her life."

I draw a deep steadying breath. "As much as I want to respect your independence, you either come with me now or I'll call your family so they can keep you company instead." I keep my voice gentle, but my words allow no argument. I'm not leaving her when she's teetering so emotionally.

"Leave," she insists.

"You're so fucking maddening, Indie," I bite out, grabbing my phone to scroll for a number. "Who should I call—Lyric or Harper?"

"Why are you doing this?"

That's a great question because this shouldn't be my problem, but when it comes to Indie everything seems to be important. This situation . . . It's killing me not knowing what to do or say. Should I search for my old therapist from college? I know how to deal with my demons, but someone else's . . . Well, that is completely out of my depth.

I squarely meet her wounded gaze. "Because I care, alright?" I force the admission out roughly. "We're friends now and I want to look after you."

I wave the phone meaningfully. "So either you come willingly or I start dialing your sisters. Your choice."

She closes her eyes and says, "Fine, I'm going but make no mistake, I'm doing this against my better judgment."

I tuck my phone away as relief hits me that she's agreed. "So I'm guessing your family doesn't actually know about . . . him." I watch her face closely. "This is why you freaked out when I asked about your need for animal companions, right?"

Ice, Love, & Other Penalties

Her jaw firms stubbornly, lips pressing into a thin line. "I said stop digging, Brynes," she repeats in a clipped tone, moving briskly to collect her shoes and Rigby's leash, clearly eager to leave. "We're going in my car since Rigby is coming along."

I open up my palm placatingly. "Sure, where are the keys?"

She glares at my hand and then at me. "I can drive."

"Humor me, darling, and give me your car keys, please," I cajole lightly, but I have no intention of letting her drive in this state.

Her eyes narrow. "Stop calling me that. We're not friends and there won't be any benefits," she bites out.

I want to argue that last part, my gaze dropping briefly to her lips before I catch myself, but after what I just found out I know I can't pursue anything further until I'm certain she's actually open to it.

"You don't get to take away the friendship card, Indie," I admonish gently. "Now let's head out, we don't have much time left." I gesture toward the door, determined to get us moving.

"What about Myra's party?"

I exhale heavily as I consider it. I don't even know if I should still have the party at this point. If Anastasia plans on fighting me for custody this could blow everything up, and I need to prepare myself and Myra for that possibility. Starting with finding a good child therapist in case things get ugly.

I huff out a mirthless laugh under my breath. When will my life ever just be quiet and normal?

Never, answers a wry voice inside my head.

It's always been a roller coaster where I look at

everyone's lives and everyone is shitting rainbows and hearts. Me, *I can't get a fucking break*, I think bitterly. When I glance at Indie, I wonder why I'm even bothering with pursuing her. She's so out of my league and even with the demons she's dealing with, she'll eventually find happiness just like the rest—and be far away from me.

"She loves unicorns," Indie says suddenly. "I can ask Teddy to make it all about unicorns—at your house."

I scrub a hand roughly over my jaw, conflicted. "We shouldn't do that. What if my sister shows up that day and makes a scene?"

"Then we'll find another place to celebrate her," Indie suggests gently. She touches my arm lightly. "Myra will still have her big party and that day you can relax and enjoy it with her, no matter what happens."

I feel myself softening under her reassuring tone and gentle touch. And even when she's so out of my league, she makes me feel like things aren't as shitty. But how long is this feeling going to linger?

It'll be gone soon. Nikki, my last girlfriend, left me when I brought Myra to our lives. She wasn't going to raise someone else's child. *Her or me*, she said. She left me the next day.

We're already on the road when Indie finally speaks up. "Is this why you said love is disappointing?"

"What?"

"Your mom doesn't seem very loving, then your sister abandoned her daughter . . ." She pauses, looking over at me searchingly. "What about your dad?"

"Who knows? I never went looking for him," I say tightly, hands gripped on the steering wheel.

"Love isn't always like that," she says gently,

reaching over to give my arm a supportive squeeze. "You just haven't found the right person yet."

Her words burrow deep within me, igniting a spark in a long-dormant corner of my heart. It's an inexplicable shift, a stirring of something unnamed yet it has been lying dormant for years—maybe an eternity. I find myself gripped by a sudden impulse to halt the relentless march of time, to stop the car and bridge the gap between us with more than just words.

The urge to pull her close, to feel the heat of her breath against my skin, to taste the truth with a kiss, becomes urgent.

But maybe I'm just reacting because I'm vulnerable and the past hour has been an exchange of emotional truths and heart-wrenching tragedies.

For a moment, I entertain the possibilities. Maybe, just maybe, she's right. Or even more terrifying and exhilarating is the thought that perhaps she's the one who can save me from a life half-lived.

Before I can think better of it, I reach over and take her hand, bringing it to my lips. I press a soft kiss to her knuckles, feeling her intake of breath.

"Indie . . ." Her name escapes me in a ragged whisper.

She gives my hand a squeeze. "It's okay," she says gently.

I run my thumb over the back of her hand, wishing I could freeze this moment. But eventually I force myself to let go, returning both hands to the wheel. We drive on in charged silence, the ghost of a kiss that hasn't happened lingering between us.

Chapter Thirty-Four

Tyberius

WHEN I LAND, I send a text to Indie, letting her know I'm in Calgary. Her response is a bit strange though. *Hey, Myra is sleeping over at my place today.*

I hesitate, thumbs hovering over my phone screen. Should I ask if she's okay? Maybe she's having another episode of anxiety. What if instead they go to her

Ice, Love, & Other Penalties

parents or . . . Can Harper be with her? I trust Indie, but I worry for her when she's overwhelmed by panic.

My first instinct is to call her. She picks up right after the first ring, her voice cool and casual. "You didn't have to call."

"Are you okay?" I ask, unable to hide my concern.

"Uh-huh. Perfectly fine," she responds. Her tone remains calm, but I detect a hint of tension.

I choose my next words carefully, not wanting to upset her. "Babe, it's okay to take Myra with you, but if you're having a hard time today I would feel better if your sisters were there too."

"The only time I freak out is when you're around—sex gives me anxiety. You're far enough so I'm perfectly fine," she states, and honestly, I'm not sure how to feel about that.

I flinch, stung even though I know she doesn't mean it personally. "Tell me how you really feel," I plead softly.

"Just did."

In that moment, Jude approaches as we head toward the waiting bus outside the private hangar. "How crazy is your mother?" he asks, his eyes wide with alarm.

I pull the phone away from my ear, shock splashing across my features from Jude's question.

Returning to my conversation with Indie, I ask, "Is my mother there?"

"She's at your house, yes. I was bringing the groceries for the next couple days. She ambushed me at your front door . . . the woman is demanding," Indie continues, irritation creeping into her tone. "I left her and the groceries outside. Didn't let her go in. And honestly . . . I don't want to take Myra back there now."

Jude's eyes narrow, his jaw clenching. "Again, how crazy is your mother?" he insists, tension radiating from him. "Do we need security? What the hell is happening? I don't like my sister and your kid being in potential danger."

"She's toxic but not dangerous," I reply tightly. "Just greedy. I agree, we should keep Myra and Indie away while I'm gone."

I raise the phone again. "You okay, Indie?"

"Totally fine," she reiterates. "She didn't scare me, but she's a little too aggressive. I literally jumped in my car and left her bitching. Although, I needed to send someone to your place to retrieve David Meowie. Hence why Jude now knows."

I wince, dread pooling in my stomach. "The Decker family gossip chain activated?"

Jude shoots me a piercing glare just as Indie confirms, "Uh-huh."

I chuckle. "You people are too fucking much."

Jude's eyes drill into me. "We'll watch your kid. You get on that bus and stay the fuck away from my sister," he growls through gritted teeth. "I don't like whatever screwed up friendship you two have going on."

The irony isn't lost on me. Before ending the call, I ask Indie quietly, "Does he know what Rossi did to you?"

Indie sucks in a sharp breath. "How do you know it was him?" she whispers.

"I had a hunch. You just confirmed," I say gently.

"No one knows and I thought we were going to

leave that alone," she replies, voice quivering. "See, you're the one who sets my anxiety into overdrive."

Guilt twists my gut. "I'm sorry, I shouldn't have brought it up," I murmur, running a hand through my hair in frustration. "I just miss you, darling. Thank you for taking care of Myra."

The words slip out before I can stop them. I shouldn't have said I miss her, but it's the truth. The fact that she had to deal with my mother upsets me deeply.

On the bus, I call my agent to give him a heads-up, even though this isn't technically his job. No surprise, he already knows—the Decker gossip train reached him too. He's dealing with my mother personally, though I dread what that entails.

AFTER THE GAME, I arrive at my hotel room to find a voicemail from my mother, one from my agent, and a text from Indie. I listen to my agent first. He sent my mother back to Florida with a restraining order after she apparently slapped Indie and threatened her. Fury boiled up inside me at the thought. Maybe it's best that I didn't know about it earlier or I would've been useless during the game.

I delete my mother's message without listening, wanting nothing more to do with her. Indie's text is an image of a tent set up in the middle of her living room. The caption says, "Sleepover."

Before I text her back, I call my agent. We discuss my mother, Myra, and how this could impact my place with the Sasquatches. As long as I stay away from the owner's sister I'm good, he claims. Well, that ship sailed.

I don't know exactly what's happening with Indie, but I want to pursue her. After the day at her house when she told me about Rossi, and I gave her a few of my own truths I knew that we needed to tread lightly to figure out what it is that's happening between the two of us. But I know it's more than just wanting to protect her.

She has learned a lot about my mother, but there're parts I haven't shared about my childhood. I will open up when I'm ready. Which is the reason why I'm starting to go back to therapy.

Langdon gives me a few more numbers to call so I can work through my issues and confide in Myra. When I try telling him that it's not so easy to tell your adoptive child that I'm not actually her father, he cuts me off. He and his husband had no issues being upfront with their kids about where they came from.

So far everyone I've talked to about that issue seems to have an unexpectedly simple perspective. I guess I have to just figure this out and tell Myra. I have to trust that the bond we've forged since I brought her into my life won't break.

Once I'm done with the call, I text Indie, *Can you talk?*

Worry creeps in as she doesn't answer soon enough. Is everything okay?

> Indie: Nope. I can't even text.

> Ty: Is everything okay?

> Indie: Yeah, but as I explained to you, we're having a sleepover—Lyr and Harp are here too.

Irritation flares up that she kept some details of the confrontation from me.

> Ty: Why didn't you tell me that my mother assaulted you?

> Indie: It was a slap on the face. I'm fine.

My jaw clenches.

> Ty: Not according to Langdon. He said Mom left red marks on your cheek.

> Indie: I'm fine, can we discuss this tomorrow?

I want to press further but decide to give in to her request.

> Ty: Fine. I'll let it go for now. Miss you.

> Indie: Congrats on that assist, see you in a couple of days.

And I can't help but send her another one.

> Ty: But you don't miss me?

> Indie: Maybe a little.

> Ty: Sweet dreams, darling.

Chapter Thirty-Five

Ty: I can't believe you left me with twelve little screaming children.

> Indie: Hey, I never promised I'd be there for the party. How bad is it?

Ty: The party is not so bad, but the moms . . . Two of them want to exchange numbers—for playdates.

> Indie: I mean Myra could benefit from more playdates.

Ty: No, honey, they want adult playdates. Like the one you owe me.

Ice, Love, & Other Penalties

> Indie: I don't owe you anything, but seriously, they're hitting on you?

> Ty: Yep. It could've been great if you had come to give me a hand—to keep these women away from me.

> Indie: Or I would've made a schedule so everyone could take turns. :wink: emoji

> Ty: It's twelve forty-five and I'm not amused, Walker.

> Indie: Sorry, Brynes, but . . . you're going to have to defend yourself today.

> Ty: Why are you not here?

> Indie: I was there yesterday morning—bright-eyed and bushy-tailed. Myra loved my present and . . . the special pancakes too. Plus I accompanied you to deliver the cupcakes to the school.

> Ty: Which I really appreciate you for that.

> Indie: Also, I took her for dinner and we played board games with Harper before she went to bed. See, I did all the things, no need to join the party.

Ty: Okay, now you're just gloating while I'm still getting insinuating glances from these women. One of them has a pretty big ring that screams "married."

Indie: Yeah, but you're a hot hockey player. Maybe one of them has you on their list.

Ty: What list?

Indie: Of people they're allowed to sleep with given the chance.

Ty: That's not a thing.

Indie: Some people do have it.

Ty: Do you?

Indie: I would need to be in a relationship to even consider it, however, I don't think it's something I would do. I'm not judging but it's not my thing.

Ty: Good—I'm what you like to call possessive.

Indie: Ugh, I see where you're going and I'm going to have to stop you right there. Enjoy your party and . . . don't collect too many phone numbers, stud.

Chapter Thirty-Six

Tyberius

AT THE END of November I realize that my life hasn't changed much from what I had in Florida. Except there's a beautiful woman who keeps me awake at night and lusting after her during the day. Knowing what Indie went through changes our dynamic. Our friendship deepens, but I keep my mouth and my hands to myself when we're in the same vicinity, no matter how strongly I want to pull her into my arms.

Before we know it, the holidays arrive. We're invited to the trimming of the tree at the Deckers' house. I have a hard time keeping up with everyone's names, but it's not impossible. Someone should give me a medal for not going all die-hard fan on . . . Well, almost all the family, I thought to myself, suppressing my inner fanboy tendencies.

The next week, we get invited to Gabe's house. I'm surprised when I learn that it's the gotcha day for Cora and Caleb, when Gabe and his wife Ameline officially adopt them. While Myra is playing with Cora in the backyard with some other friends, Indie approaches me, with a hesitant but determined look on her face.

"Have you thought about telling her, yet?" she asks.

I glance at her, unable to stop my eyes from drifting down her body. She looks so beautiful I can barely stand it. I want nothing more than to pull her into my arms and kiss her senseless. But I resist the urge—somebody give me a fucking medal.

"Have you talked to your therapist?" I ask instead, deflecting her question. I can't tell Myra anything until I know Indie is ready.

She gives me a suspicious look, eyes narrowing. "Why are you so insistent?"

"Other than I think it will help you?" I say. "I'm fucking selfish and I would like my benefits back if you don't mind?" I grin, trying to lighten the suddenly serious mood.

"Focus on your child," she retorts, giving me an unamused look.

And that's when my child approaches me. "Daddy,

can you meet a mom who wants to adopt me?" she asks eagerly.

"Excuse me?" I almost choke on my own saliva.

Indie covers her mouth, but I can see those brown eyes dancing with amusement.

"A mom," Myra repeats. "I want a mom. Cora got a new one and a dad too."

"See, pretty simple," Indie states, lips quirking.

Myra gives her a sweet smile and those doe eyes open wide. "Would you like to adopt me and be my mom?"

In that moment, Jacob Decker walks by and flashes me a stern, warning look that makes me gulp. "Go and look for someone else to fulfill that role. My child is off-limits."

I lift my palms in surrender, taking a nervous step back. No way I was messing with a protective Jacob Decker.

Indie squats down to Myra's level and whispers something that makes Myra nod happily. She turns to Jacob with an angelic smile. "Can I have some more cake, please, Mr. Decker?"

"What exactly did you tell her to do?" I ask Indie suspiciously.

She shrugs, a secretive smile playing on her lips. "Nothing."

"But you did," I persist, narrowing my eyes at her.

"I'm just keeping him away before he starts badgering you. You're welcome," she says casually. Then she turns on her heel and walks away, hips swaying enticingly.

I watch her go, desire burning through me. My eyes trace over her body, lingering on her curves and remembering the feel of her in my arms. I want her, badly. But until she's ready for more, I have to restrain myself no matter how difficult it is. I let out a frustrated breath and drag my gaze away before I give in to temptation. I know the wait will be worth it.

"I don't know how I let you convince me to come with you," Indie complains as I'm driving toward my house. "Anyone could've dropped me later so I can get my car from your garage."

"It's fair since you helped Myra convince me to let her stay for a sleepover," I claim with a grin. "What happened to no sleepovers until they're seven?"

"Are you complaining about tonight or tomorrow night?" she asks wryly. "I'm the one who'll be dealing with a horde of little girls, not you."

"Your sisters are coming to help," I remind her, glancing her way. The late afternoon sun caresses her skin, highlighting her beauty. I force my eyes back on the road.

"No, all the Decker girls will be invading," she says. I don't have to look to know she's grinning.

"It's funny that you're still the Decker girls," I point out.

"Our families call us that, no matter how many times we tell them we're all grown up—why fight the system?" she responds. "Thank you for letting us take over your house."

"Thank you for welcoming Myra into your family," I respond earnestly, taking her hand and brushing a kiss

Ice, Love, & Other Penalties

over her knuckles. Her breath catches at the contact, giving me hope. "So, therapy?"

"I actually switched therapists. I wasn't comfortable telling my old one what happened to me. It felt wrong," she responds, gazing out the window. "It's . . . a step. Recognizing what really happened and finding a way to stop blaming myself. I refused to be the victim so I decided to do things under my terms."

"It always has to be under your terms," I say with a small smile, eyes on the road.

"No. I think there has to be something more . . . like communication and mutual respect," she argues.

I simply hum in response. We drive in comfortable silence the rest of the way. Finally, I pull into the garage at my house, the motion sensor lights flickering on to chase away the growing dusk. I shift into Park and turn off the ignition, but make no move to exit. There's something I need to say first.

"I'm proud of you, Indie," I tell her gently. "I know how hard this is."

"Because someday you might be able to ask for your benefits back?" she asks, one eyebrow raised.

"No, because you're finally taking charge of your life," I state, turning in my seat to face her fully. "I only want you to be okay."

"Why?" she asks, brows furrowed in confusion.

I want to say, *Because I love you, because between you showing up that first morning when I was desperate and afraid of what my future would look like in this city and this moment, I've fallen completely and hopelessly for you.*

But neither of us are ready for something that big though. So instead, I reach out and tuck a stray lock of hair behind her ear, my fingers trailing lightly, yearningly over her cheek. "Because you deserve to be happy, Indie," I say softly. "And I'll do anything I can to help you get there."

Her breath catches at my gentle touch and the tender look in my eyes. For a long moment we stay suspended like that, gazes locked, faces inches apart. The air between us seems to hum. Then, as if drawn together by an invisible thread, we both start to lean in.

My eyelids drift shut as her lips meet mine, soft and seeking at first, then firmer and more passionate. My heart pounds wildly in my chest as we kiss. One of my hands slides around to cradle the back of her head, tangling in her hair, as I pull her closer.

She makes a small, breathy sound against my mouth that sends desire rocketing through me. Her hands clutch at my shoulders, then travel up to frame my face as the kiss deepens further. In this perfect, private moment there is nothing and no one else in the world but me and her.

Chapter Thirty-Seven

Indigo

My lips still tingle from that earth-shattering kiss as we make our way into Ty's house. I sneak a glance at him out of the corner of my eye, my heart skipping a little when I find him already looking at me. The heat in his gaze makes my cheeks flush.

I'm not quite sure how we got from the garage to

here, it was a bit of a daze. The kiss replays over and over in my mind—the way his mouth slanted over mine, firm and seeking at first, then more passionate as we both gave in to the attraction simmering between us.

Ty reaches out and takes my hand, entwining our fingers and brushing a soft, swoon-worthy kiss over my knuckles that makes my insides melt.

"I don't want you to leave tonight." His thumb grazes my cheekbone, a question in his eyes. "But I also don't want you to think that I brought you here to . . ."

"Claim your benefits?" I supply, cheeks flushing.

He winces. "I just want to spend time with you. We're always on the run, or Myra is around."

"What if I want to give you a benefit or two?" I tease, hiding my own nervousness, or hoping that we don't get too personal.

I mean even when I try to avoid it, we always end up talking about our past, or the future—which isn't too special. He just wants to get through as many seasons as possible because after that he won't have the same income. Me . . . there's the business I'm trying to start up with Lyr and Harper, but it'll take time.

Neither one of us is ready for it. Next semester, I'm going to start taking business classes. Lyr is compiling some designs and Harp is still not sure if she can even work as a biochemist because her stupid ex-fiancé made her sign a non-competitive contract that stops her from working on anything in her field for a long time.

But I do know a lot of Ty's past now. How he got his first skates from the coach of an outreach program, and that he now donates part of his earnings to places like that. He believes hockey and that program saved him from an uncertain future.

Ice, Love, & Other Penalties

I love that I know those little things about him that no one else does. But it's knowing these details that scares me a lot more than having sex with him. Getting close is . . . what if I lose myself and this time I end up like my bio-mom?

Ty's hands close gently over mine, bringing me back to this moment, to us.

"As much as part of me wants that—benefits and sexual favors—what I want more is to just talk with you tonight." He presses a soft kiss to my wrist. "There's still so much I don't know."

My chest constricts. "Intimacy scares me," I remind him.

He nods. "I know. And isn't that what life's all about? Doing what scares you the most, conquering your demons."

I gulp and nod once. "Letting you touch me could be a good way to claim something too."

"Somehow I think you're more afraid of opening your soul than your legs, darling," Ty says bluntly.

"That's crude," I mutter, cheeks flushing with embarrassment.

"No, it's the truth," Ty insists, gaze unwavering.

"I trusted him, you know?" I say, not sure if it's a way to explain why this is as much as he can get or . . . I don't know why I'm doing it, but I continue, "With everything. He knew my fears and my dreams. I let him in too deep and then . . . gave him something I thought he'd cherish. It's hard to trust again. And you . . . You're temporary. We both agreed that's what this is. I'd prefer to go to your living room and let you fuck me than tell you my secrets."

"Then, we'll watch a movie," he proposes.

"What?"

"We can play a board game?"

"I don't understand," I state in confusion. "I'm offering anything, a blow job, fucking me anyway you want, and your answer is . . . let's play a board game?"

He nods. "You're not ready to give me what I really want, and I won't push you."

I'm horny and burning from the inside out after the kiss he gave me. I need a release. I'm soaking wet, ready to . . . do anything, and he's rejecting me?

"But—"

"Honestly, I think you want to find a new way to disappear from me. I won't let you," he states.

"Tyberius, be reasonable," I argue.

"I heard there's a new rom-com streaming," he says, walking toward the family room.

"You're insufferable." I walk after him.

"You're maddening, but maybe that's one of my favorite things about you. I love how you make up your mind and it's hard to convince you that there are other ways."

I halt in my tracks. "What do you mean by that?"

Ty glances over his shoulder. "Is there a problem with your hearing? Or was I speaking too fast?"

"You . . . You shouldn't have favorite things about me or . . . I—" I press my lips together. "Don't make this difficult, please. I really like you and Myra. She needs stability and I'm the only one who can give it to her right now."

"Some things can't be helped," he says.

"I have to go."

"Indie," he calls after me, but I'm running toward the garage. "Babe, stop."

"No," I say, as I jump in my car making sure my purse and keys are inside. "We said no feelings, Ty."

"I couldn't help myself and I won't apologize for it. Or for loving you," he states and my heart stutters when I hear that, and still, I leave.

This—emotions and . . . love. I can't handle it. More so from a guy like him. Someone who cares too much and gives his everything to those he loves. What if I let myself fall and then he leaves? It'll destroy me.

WHEN I GET HOME. I run to my bedroom and take a shower to calm down. I wish Rigby were here but it seemed so easy to leave him with Myra. How stupid is that?

After I put on my pajamas and dry my hair, I look at my phone. There's a text from Ty, *at least tell me you got home safe, please.*

I should ignore him, but since I don't want him to drive by, I respond, *I'm here.*

> Ty: Are Rigby and Dave with you?

> Indie: Remember we left Rig at Gabe's? Dave is here though.

> Ty: I can go and get him for you.

> Indie: I don't want to see you.

> Ty: I can't believe you're mad because I'm falling in love with you.

Indie: Stop saying that.

Ty: It makes you uncomfortable?

Indie: It scares me because what if I fall and then you don't catch me?

Ty: What if we fall for each other and we enjoy the rest of our lives together?

Indie: Have I ever told you about my biological parents?

Ty: No.

Indie: It's pretty simple really. Dad died and Mom couldn't live without him. She was twenty-five weeks pregnant when she killed herself. I almost died too.

Ty: I'm sorry.

Indie: My biggest fear is love—romantic love. One of the things I've been discovering about the Frederick incident is that after he left, I was afraid that I would do what my mother did to herself. Obviously, I have PTSD because he raped me but add to that what happened with my bio-parents and . . . I'm pretty fucked up.

Ice, Love, & Other Penalties

Ty: I'm sorry to hear about your parents, but you can't stop living or wanting to have someone to share your life with.

Indie: You scare me too.

Ty: What can I do so you can trust me? I would never hurt you.

Indie: Yeah, but what if I lose you and I lose myself after that?

Ty: You can't live in fear.

Indie: You keep saying that.

Ty: I do because I know what it's like to be anxious about the future due to your childhood experiences. Mom and I lived in poverty. The only food we got was when she had someone to support her. We didn't have a house, only a car. Sometimes we would stay in shitty hotels, or with whoever she was fucking. There was the occasional shelter during the winter. I got to eat because of the school programs, but it wasn't enough. Once Anastasia came into the picture, I did a few things I'm not proud of to ensure she had baby food. Since I left for college I've lived with the fear that I could end up in that same place. That no matter how much money I make, one day everything I've worked for will disappear and I'll go back to living in a car with my daughter.

> Indie: That'd be impossible. You're pretty frugal and a hard worker.

Ty: The fear is still there, and now I'm working hard to understand the why and stop myself from living a miserable life. I don't want this to affect Myra or any future children we have.

> Indie: We're quite a pair.

Ice, Love, & Other Penalties

> Indie: Wait, children we have? Who is this we you're talking about?

> Ty: You and me, babe. I love you. For the first time, I can see a future that doesn't include playing until my knees give up and saving up for my child's college. I want to have a family, you—a woman who understand me even when she's stubborn as fuck. And if I have to wait years until you can open up to me, I'm fine with it.

> Indie: Find someone less broken.

> Ty: Or, and hear me out because this is a brilliant idea. We can fuse our shattered pieces and make a whole heart out of them.

> Indie: Stop. I'm going to have a hard time tonight—panic attacks and nightmares and . . .

The doorbell rings, making me jump. When I open the door, Ty is there with Rigby next to him.

"We're here to keep you company tonight—so there are no panic attacks or nightmares," he says as if that makes it okay to be at my house.

My lip quivers. *Don't give in,* I order myself.

"You were texting and driving?" I chide him.

He shakes his head. "Nah, I went to pick up Rig as soon as you left my place. I might've gone a little faster than the limit to make it back when you did."

"Why didn't you just drop him off? Why text me

and . . ." I show him the phone as if accusing him of doing something atrocious. Like opening his heart to me and making me confess things I don't want to.

"You seem to have less trouble talking to me when we text," he responds, leaning closer and kissing my nose and then my lips.

"We're not having sex," I say, hoping that will keep him away.

"That's okay. As long as you let me be with you until I have to leave in the morning."

"Don't do this, Ty, please," I beg him.

"Love you?"

I nod. "Yeah."

"You seem to be ready for bed. Why don't we go upstairs? I promise not to fall more in love with you tonight," he says, but that smirk on his lips tells me that it'd be impossible to keep that promise.

"We can have tea and then you leave," I propose.

He nods. "Let's have tea and see what happens afterwards." He winks at me and I have the feeling that he's not going to leave tonight.

Well, I hope the couch is comfortable because I don't plan on sharing my bed with him. Nope.

Chapter Thirty-Eight

Indigo

I feel his fingers curl around my hip, pulling me closer to him. His free hand runs down my spine, sending shivers through my body. I gasp as his thumb brushes against my sensitive flesh, causing my eyes to close involuntarily. I lean into his touch, wanting more.

You shouldn't have let him sleep in with you, but we were so tired, I respond to myself, grinding my hips closer to him, wanting to reach for his hard cock and just ride him. But I don't move, I just let him do anything to me.

He kisses my neck, his lips soft against my skin. His teeth graze my earlobe, sending a shiver down my spine. I moan softly, unable to resist the wave of desire that washes over me.

"Do you like that?" His voice is rough, full of emotion.

I nod, unable to speak. His fingers continue their slow massage against my skin, moving up and down my spine. I can feel the tension in my body start to ease as the pleasure builds.

"You're so responsive," he whispers, his breath hot against my ear. "I could spend all night making love to you."

"Ty, fuck me," I moan.

"You want me to fuck you hard, little minx? Fill you up, make you mine?" His throaty voice makes every cell of my body quiver.

The thought of him stretching me, possessing me sends a jolt of excitement through me. I want him to spend all night here, making love, exploring every inch of each other's bodies. But we can't . . . not yet.

I'm not ready for him, for us. Will I ever be?

"We shouldn't," I murmur, trying to keep my voice steady.

He pulls back slightly, looking into my eyes. "Why not?"

Because we're not ready, I want to say.

He kisses me again, this time more passionately. His hand moves from my back to my breast, gently cupping it through my shirt. I gasp at the sensation, my body responding instinctively.

"Tell me to stop," he whispers against my lips. "Tell me you don't want this."

I shake my head, unable to speak. He smiles, his green eyes dark with desire. And then he leans in, his lips finding mine in a slow, sensual kiss.

I respond eagerly, opening my mouth to him. His tongue sweeps inside, tangling with mine in a dance of passion. I feel my heart racing, my body on fire. This is what I've been miss-

ing, what I've been craving. And he's the one who can give it to me.

The sound of water running fills the room, breaking the intense moment. We pull apart, both of us breathing heavily. He stands up.

"Don't go," I beg him.

And suddenly, I open my eyes with a gasp, disoriented. The dream-Ty fades as I take in the familiar surroundings of my bedroom. Early morning light filters through the shutters and the shower runs in my adjoining bathroom. I sit up slowly, pressing my fingers to still-tingling lips. Just a dream . . . Yet, it felt so real. My heart continues to pound as traces of the dream mixed with desire and disappointment wash over me.

The water shuts off and the bathroom door opens. Ty steps out, a towel hanging low on his hips, rippled muscles still dripping from the shower.

"Are you okay, babe?" he asks, brow furrowed in concern.

"Uh-huh," I murmur, shaken. I press a hand to my chest, trying to slow my racing pulse.

"You were screaming," he says, coming to sit on the edge of the bed. His warm hand smooths back my tangled hair. "Bad dream?"

I lick my still-tingling lips, avoiding his probing gaze. "I guess so," I hedge, the passionate dream lover's identity hitting me fully. My cheeks flush. I meet Ty's eyes, seeing the same smoldering desire from the dream reflected there.

He laughs, a knowing glint in his eyes. "Your cheeks are flushing . . . Somehow, I think you had a very good dream. Was I there?"

"No," I lie unconvincingly.

His grin widens. "Was it good?"

I give a noncommittal shrug, squirming under his playful scrutiny, heart still racing.

He brushes his knuckles tenderly down my cheek. "Soon, I promise," he murmurs. Though his tone is light, there's an undercurrent of longing that mirrors my own.

I lean into his touch despite myself. "Soon," I echo in a whisper. His thumb caresses my lower lip and my breath catches. As our eyes lock, the air charges between us. Soon may not come soon enough.

Buoyed up by reckless desire, I stand abruptly and grip the edge of his towel. His eyebrows shoot up in surprise, but he doesn't move to stop me as I give the towel a firm tug. It falls to the floor, leaving him gloriously bare before me.

A thrill courses through me at my own daring, along with a healthy appreciation for what the towel no longer conceals. I let my gaze travel slowly over him. I kneel between his legs, feeling the heat radiating off his skin. He watches me, his eyes dark with desire. I trace my fingers along the length of his cock, feeling the veins pulsing beneath my touch. I can't help but wonder what it would be like to have him inside of me.

"You want this?" he asks, his voice rough with need.

I nod, my heart racing at the thought of taking him into my mouth. He groans, the sound vibrating through my body as I lean forward and take him. His taste is salty and sweet, with a hint of arousal. I take him deeper, feeling the muscles in his abdomen tense as I do so.

My tongue darts out to trace the vein on the underside of his shaft, and I hear him gasp. I look up at him, catching his gaze. The fire in his eyes sends shivers down my spine. His hips thrust, giving me better access.

I take him as deep as I can, feeling him hit the back of my throat. He groans loudly, his fingers digging into the skin of his thighs.

I pull back, slowly sliding my mouth off his cock. I look up at him, our gazes locked. He's breathing heavily, his chest rising and falling rapidly. I lean forward, taking his cock back into my mouth and swirling my tongue around the head. I hear him moan, "Indie, please," the plea sounding through my bedroom.

I continue to pleasure him with my mouth, using my hands to stroke his thighs and balls, teasing him with gentle squeezes. He's losing control, his hips bucking wildly as he tries to get closer to his release. I increase the pressure on his cock, taking him deeper into my throat.

He lets out another strangled cry, his hips bucking wildly. I increase the pressure, sliding my tongue along the sensitive ridge.

His fingers dig into my shoulders, leaving bruises, but I don't mind. This is what I want. I want him to feel everything. I take him deeper into my mouth, feeling him hit the back of my throat. He groans loudly. I continue to pleasure him, using my hands to stroke and massage him. His body tenses, and I know he's close. I swirl my tongue around the head, tasting the salty mixture of sweat and arousal.

He cries out, his voice hoarse. I feel his cock twitch, pulsing with his imminent release. I take him as deep as I can, feeling the warmth spread through my body as he comes. I swallow every drop, feeling it slide down my throat. As he catches his breath, I look up at him, our gazes locked. He's flushed, his chest heaving. I smile, knowing I did that to him this time—not to prove I have power over him, but because I genuinely want him.

"I'll be thinking of that while I'm away," he murmurs, as he helps me stand up and takes me into his arms, "missing you."

He kisses me deeply and I melt into him, threading my fingers through his hair. When we finally break for air, he rests his forehead against mine.

"I think I fell even more in love with you, if that's possible," he says. His voice catches slightly on the word *love* as if he still can't believe this is real.

But I'm the one who might not be able to catch up to him who is scared of whatever happens next because this time I wouldn't only lose the guy, but also his little girl.

Chapter Thirty-Nine

> Ty: On the plane, officially thirty-one thousand feet above sea level. And guess what? I miss you already.

> Indie: So, the blow job worked, huh?

> Ty: You did it so I would miss you?

> Indie: No, I . . . Do you know that a blow job is more intimate sometimes than penetration?

> Ty: Today I believe it. Thank you for that little piece of yourself.

> Indie: How is it that you always know what to say?

> Ty: Only with you. What's the plan for today? I mean, other than missing me.

Indie: I got a call from Gabe asking if I could take the girls to the zoo.

> Ty: Are you going to?

Indie: Yeah, they need a break from their children and guests. Having twins is not for the faint of heart. Fortunately, Coda is coming with me. I'll make sure to take pics of Myra and her favorite animals.

> Ty: Instead of just sending me pictures of the zoo, send me selfies too so I miss you less.

Indie: Ha, we'll see. I'm going to shower, get dressed and swing by your house to pick up some fun clothes for her.

> Ty: I'm going to pretend that I understand that statement. By the way, did Lyric mean the whole you're going to start your own company and leave me?

Indie: We're looking into it, yes. I won't leave Myra until we find a nanny for her.

> Ty: Are you moving to New York or Paris?

Ice, Love, & Other Penalties

Indie: Neither. We'll be doing everything here, but obviously at times they'll have to travel. Not me. I'm happy here.

Ty: But last night you told me why you came back from New York.

Indie: I regret falling asleep while telling you about my life. But to be honest, I prefer to stay in Seattle. If I leave, I won't be able to visit my family as often and I'll miss my murky weather.

Ty: What if I take you to a sunny place during the summertime?

Indie: Stop making plans with me.

Ty: For now, since I have to watch some plays and . . . your brother isn't as laid-back as he looks.

Indie: He's not. Have fun with him. I'm on my way out to pick up the little ones.

Ty: Thank you for doing that.

Chapter Forty

> Indie: My grandparents want to know if you guys will be spending Christmas with us.

Ty: I would love to, but I promised Myra that I would take her to the beach—got the tickets back in July.

> Indie: Know you'll be missed.

Ty: By you?

> Indie: The family, obviously. Me . . . I could care less.

Ty: I can buy you a ticket and take you with us.

Ice, Love, & Other Penalties

> Indie: And miss Christmas with the Deckers? Nope. It's a magical holiday no one should miss. The artificial pond is going up next week. We'll be ice-skating and drinking hot cocoa all day long.

> Ty: Of course you have a pond and a magical Christmas. How was the zoo?

> Indie: Fun. We're currently making ice cream sandwiches with the cookies we baked earlier.

> Ty: My kid will be bouncing off the walls with that much sugar, good luck.

> Indie: Good luck to you tomorrow evening when you're back on daddy-duty—and I'll be gone.

> Ty: Check your calendar, babe. I won't be back until Tuesday.

> Indie: Great. I was looking at the wrong week. In any case, I have to go back to the kitchen.

> Ty: Miss you.

Chapter Forty-One

Tyberius

It's one of those odd Sundays that Indie is skipping brunch with her parents and the whole Sunday gatherings with the Deckers to be with us. I still can't believe I convinced her to spend the day with us. I want to think that it's because next week we're leaving for Cabo San Lucas for a couple of days and we won't be spending

Christmas with her. A stupid, hopeful part of me thinks she'll miss us while we're gone.

The reality might be that my child was able to convince her to finally join us for the brunch she owes us since . . . she came into our life.

Even though Indie's house is smaller than ours, it's cozier and sometimes feels more like a home. The couple of times I've mentioned it to her, she insists mine would feel the same if I finish furnishing it.

Is she right? Who knows? I don't need a library or a media room, or . . . I should look for a house that feels more like mine and less like a prompt of a sitcom. Maybe that's something I will do when the season is over and I get to take a break. Look for a place that will be good for my family. I glance up at Indie and grin like an idiot thinking—our family.

Indie's eyes narrow suspiciously. "Whatever you're thinking is a no," she says flatly.

"You're not part of my new plan," I lie unconvincingly.

She chuckles, glancing at the sea of papers, markers, and two steaming mugs of coffee in front of Indie and me. Myra sits with her crayons scattered around, her tongue peeking out slightly as she deliberates over her masterpiece. She's taking the after-school art classes very seriously and even wants us to take her to more museums so she can learn more styles—whatever that is.

"We're not going on some expedition," Indie says firmly, shaking her head. "It's too cold outside."

My eyes glance between Indie and Myra, the two centers of my universe. Do we need to go anywhere?

Not as long as they're here, but we definitely need a plan for us.

"What if before dinner we go on a drive to look at Christmas displays?" I suggest.

Myra's face lights up. "Yes. I'd love that," she exclaims. "Maybe next year we should go to a mountain for Christmas."

"Let's get through this holiday first," I reply, thinking that in a few months I hope to convince Indie to date me. If we become serious, we'll make those decisions together.

"Okay, how about a treasure hunt instead?" Myra suggests, her imagination running wild. "We can have a picnic afterwards," she adds enthusiastically.

Indie taps her chin thoughtfully. "It's too wet out for that, but we could organize an indoor hunt at your place. The picnic can be in your basement where there's artificial turf."

I look at her confused. "There's artificial turf in my basement?"

"Have you been down there?"

I shrug sheepishly. "Maybe once or twice."

Indie shakes her head in disbelief. "Seriously, why did you buy the place?"

"It was one of the only houses available at the time. You said it was discounted," I explain with a shrug. She looks at me expectantly, waiting for the real reason. "Okay, the truth is that I was worried I'd have to live in my car if I didn't choose something quickly."

To my surprise, Indie stands up, kisses my cheek, and pulls me into a hug. "If I had known you back then, I would have handled it differently," she says softly.

Ice, Love, & Other Penalties

I slip my arm around her waist, pulling her closer, and leaning my forehead against her shoulder. "It's not your fault. But maybe it isn't the right house for me after all."

"You could make it yours," Indie insists. "When I first saw it, I thought it had potential. With two or three kids, they'd have a blast there."

"You did?" I glance at her and she nods.

"Maybe you can show me your vision," I suggest.

"Are you sure you don't want to be my mom?" Myra suddenly asks Indie. "You're nice. I like you. Daddy likes you, and we're friends."

Indie tenses at the question. I immediately release her, knowing how much this freaks her out. It's not that she doesn't want us, but rather fears losing us.

"Why don't we focus on the treasure hunt and picnic instead?" I say, hoping to redirect the conversation. "Since Indie can plan it, you and I will hunt through the house. I'm not sure I even know it that well. Do you, Myra?"

"I do," Myra answers. "Indie and I play hide-and-seek here a lot, more so when Cora and Caleb visit."

"And no one has ever invited me to play?" I pretend to pout.

"Not when you're busy playing hockey all the time, Daddy," Myra retorts with a glance at Indie. "We could do hide-and-seek instead of a treasure hunt. That way you can hide too."

"We could combine both," Indie suggests brightly. "Let's gather some things and head over to your place."

Soon we arrive at the house. The morning disappears in eager preparations—maps are hand-drawn, clues written out, a 'treasure chest' stuffed with goodies.

"Where do you come up with all these creative ideas?" I ask Indie admiringly.

"Mom and my aunts always had something planned to entertain us," she responds. "As you know, my dad and his siblings are triplets, and they are pretty close. They decided to build their homes next to each other and share a backyard. They wanted us to grow up like siblings. They always had something planned for us so we wouldn't be destroying the houses—not that it stopped some of my cousins or my brothers from trying."

"And your dad and uncles didn't join in or help?" I ask, curious.

"The dads helped out sometimes, but mostly gave music lessons—that was Dad and Uncle Mattie's thing. Uncle Mason handled the martial arts training." Indie shakes her head in amusement. "With sixteen kids running around, they divided and conquered."

I can't imagine having such a big family. Handling sixteen kids seems impossible. I have enough trouble with just one. Well, that's not entirely true. Since Indie came into our lives, things between Myra and me have changed dramatically. I've become a better parent—I no longer just give in to Myra's every wish. And in turn, her behavior has improved tremendously.

When I look up at Indie I simply say, "Thank you for being a part of our lives. I don't know how our little family survived without you before."

Indie blushes beautifully at the compliment. "You guys were doing just fine. But I'm happy I could help."

But fine is not enough. This—happy—is what I want though. Sharing everything with her. If only I can convince her that we can happen.

Chapter Forty-Two

Ty: How's Christmas with the parents?

Indie: Fun, as usual. How's Cabo?

Ty: Sunny and . . . there's not much sand, but at least my girl got to spend some time on the beach like we used to when we lived in Florida.

Indie: She misses it, huh?

Ty: Surprisingly not as much as I thought. I think she missed the quality time we spent together which I'm giving to her now— thanks to your advice.

Ice, Love, & Other Penalties

> Indie: You don't give yourself enough credit. The transition between one state to the other, plus her going from a toddler to a big girl, happened at the same time. The adjustment was hard, but you two are on the other side.

Ty: You helped us, you're just afraid of being part of the equation.

> Indie: A little.

Ty: How's therapy?

> Indie: We're back to claiming the benefits?

Ty: The only benefit I want is your complete trust. That we can cuddle whenever I want, and you accept that I love you. I love eating your pussy and when you let me fuck your mouth . . . Honestly, I just want every part of you. Heart. Body. Soul.

> Indie: I'm working on it.

Ty: :grinning: emoji

> Indie: What's that for?

Ty: You're not rejecting me, I call it progress.

> Indie: I told my parents last night.

Ty: A little more context will help me understand what we're talking about.

Indie: Frederick.

Ty: Oh.

Indie: Dad wants to kill him. Mom asked if we could all go to therapy so they can work on it and also help me.

Ty: I'm glad you're finally talking about your fears with those who love you.

Indie: It's scary, but I do want to get better.

Ty: Anything I can do for you? I'll be happy to go to couples therapy.

Indie: We're not together.

Ty: Not yet. :wink: emoji

Indie: And with that, I leave you. Have a wonderful Christmas and send a kiss to Myra. I really miss her.

Ty: We miss you too.

Chapter Forty-Three

Indie: You okay?

Ty: Yeah, why?

Indie: That hit during the third period was . . . bad.

Ty: I'm fine, no worries.

Indie: Well, when you arrive home, I'll make sure to ice your shoulder.

Ty: The benefits of playing in Portland. We fly back home the same night and you'll be waiting for me.

Indie: Don't get too excited.

Ty: Oh, but we're very excited.

> Indie: We?

Ty: My cock is hoping that you'll be welcoming him too.

> Indie: Come home safe, we'll discuss your welcome home later, okay?

Chapter Forty-Four

Tyberius

When I arrive at the house, I find Indie already in the foyer, welcoming me with a smile that sends shivers down my spine. "Welcome home," she utters, her voice carrying a husky, seductive undertone.

Without waiting for another word, I pull her close, my arm snaking around her waist, and our lips crash together in a fierce, passionate kiss. It's intense, both of us stealing each other's breaths in a heated exchange, surrendering completely to the moment. When we finally break apart, we're gasping, the air around us charged with electricity.

Indie's cheeks are flushed, her eyes bright with a playful, mischievous spark. "Looks like someone's really missed this place," she teases, her voice provocative. Her smirk says it all. "Show me just how much."

Her smirk is infectious, and I can't resist mirroring it. "You've been teasing me for days," I point out, my voice dropping to a low, rough timbre. "I'm here to find out if you're everything I've imagined."

Indie's response is immediate; her warm hands land on my chest, tracing the rapid beat of my heart through my shirt. "You think you can handle what I have to offer?" she challenges, her gaze piercing.

Closing the gap, I whisper directly into her ear, my breath a soft tease. "I want all of you," I confess. "I want to find out if you're as unforgettable as I've imagined." The shiver that courses through her tells me I've struck a chord, and the air between us crackles with anticipation.

As we kiss, my mind wanders to all the places we could go from here. The possibilities are endless, and I find myself getting lost in the moment. I run my fingers through her hair, feeling the silky strands slip between my fingers. She moans into my mouth, and I know I'm on the right track. Slowly, I begin to unbutton her shirt, taking my time to expose her perfect skin to the cool air. Her breath hitches as I run my hands up her sides, tracing the delicate lines of her rib cage.

I lean down, pressing my lips down against the soft skin of her neck, and I can feel her pulse racing beneath them. With one final push, I manage to get her shirt off, revealing her lacy black bra. I take a deep breath, trying to calm myself down. This is happening so fast, but I don't want it to stop.

She looks up at me, her eyes sparkling with excitement, and I know we are both on the same page. I continue to kiss her, my hands moving up her sides toward her bra clasp. With a gentle tug, I free it and her breasts spill out. I pause for a moment, taking in the sight of her perfect breasts. My heart hammers against my chest.

As we come together, her breath against my skin is exhilarating, sending waves of shivers cascading down my spine. Her lips meet mine with an intensity that feels like she's trying to devour me, each movement deliberate, leaving no room for thought, only feeling. My heart thunders in my chest as I draw her even closer, my arms locking around her waist in a firm embrace.

She moans softly, her body arching against mine. Her taste lingers on my lips, her skin velvety under my touch. Pulling away from the kiss, I trail my lips down her neck and over her collarbone. Indie whimpers, her fingers tangling in my hair. Gently, I remove her pants, revealing her perfect body.

A groan escapes me as I kiss my way back up her body until I reach her earlobe. "You're so beautiful," I murmur, nipping gently at it. Indie shivers, her breath hitching in her throat.

"Tyberius," she breathes, barely above a whisper.

Unable to resist any longer, I pull her close and

cradle her in my arms, taking her breast into my mouth. She cries out, fingers digging into my shoulders as I suckle greedily. Her heart pounds against my chest in sync with mine.

Sliding my hand between us, I tease her wetness before slowly pushing a finger inside her. Indie gasps, hips arching off the bed. Moving in rhythm with her pleasure, I continue as she moans my name and trembles with delight. The desire for connection overwhelms me; kissing up her neck and along her jawline until our mouths meet once more feels like coming home.

Our tongues tangle as we explore each other's mouths; bodies moving in perfect sync as soft moans fill the room. Pushing another finger inside triggers a cry from Indie; nails dig into my shoulders as need courses through us both. Panting heavily after pulling away from the kiss, I whisper hoarsely, "Indie . . . I want you so much." Her eyes meet mine filled with desire and something deeper than lust.

I break away from the kiss, breathless. She looks at me with those piercing brown eyes, and I feel like I'm falling into an abyss. "You're unbelievable," I whisper.

She smirks, her voice low and seductive. "You have no idea." She steps back, and for a moment, I feel a stab of loss. But then she reaches for my pants, her fingers dancing along the zipper. With a swift motion, she pulls them down, revealing my hard cock straining against my boxers.

HER EYES WIDEN SLIGHTLY, and she licks her lips. "Well, then," she murmurs, her voice husky with desire. "It looks like you're definitely ready to play." With that, she

Ice, Love, & Other Penalties

grabs my shirt and yanks it over my head, revealing my torso. Her touch is like tiny sparks, igniting a fire within me.

She steps back, assessing me with her piercing eyes. "Mmm," she hums, her fingers tracing the muscles along my abdomen. "Not bad for a guy who just got manhandled during a game." She smirks, and I can't help but laugh.

But before I can respond, she grabs my hand, pulling me toward the couch. "Come on," she purrs. "Let's see what else you've got." I follow her lead, my heart pounding in my chest. This woman is like a drug to me, and I can't get enough.

As I watch her, my heart races. She's breathtaking, every inch of her. I can feel my cock twitching in anticipation, aching for her touch. She turns to face me, her eyes locked on mine. There's a fire in them that mirrors the heat burning within me. Without saying a word, she steps closer and trails her fingers down my chest, sending shivers down my spine.

I groan softly as she continues her descent, skimming over my abs and lower, stopping just short of my rapidly hardening cock. Her lips curve into a smirk, and she leans in slowly, her warm breath teasing the sensitive skin of my erection.

"You're already so hard for me," she whispers, her voice husky with desire. "I can't wait to feel you inside me."

Her words send a jolt of electricity through my body, making every muscle tense with anticipation. Without hesitation, she wraps her hand around my cock, giving it a firm squeeze. I gasp at the sensation, my head spinning with pleasure.

"I do love your lips wrapped around my length, but I hope you'll let me be inside you," I state.

She looks at me, frozen.

"But we're doing whatever you feel comfortable with," I correct my previous statement.

I gaze down at her. Her eyes are filled with a mix of desire and trepidation, and it's intoxicating. I can't help but lean down and capture her lips in a slow, passionate kiss, my hands roaming over her soft skin. I pull back slightly, my breathing ragged.

"What do you want?" I ask, my voice hoarse with need. "Because once we cross this line, there's no going back." She nods, her hair falling across her face.

"I know," she whispers. "But I want this, Ty. I want you inside me."

I take her in my arms, lifting her up so our bodies align perfectly. I slide inside her slowly and carefully, watching for any sign of discomfort on her face.

She meets my gaze. Love and trust fill her eyes. That look. It hits me right in the chest. Knowing that I'm not alone in this, that I'm not falling for her while she's just waiting for me to leave is everything.

She's everything.

"Ty," she breathes, wrapping her legs around me.

I groan as the feeling of her tight warm body enveloping me becomes more than I can bear. I begin to move—first slowly then with growing intensity—our rhythm matching each other perfectly.

I thrust my hips forward, burying my cock between her legs harder, deeper. Her moans become louder and louder.

I feel her inner muscles starting to flutter around me, her breath catching on increasingly loud moans.

She trembles and shakes right on the precipice. With one final deep thrust, she shatters, crying out her ecstasy. I capture her mouth in a searing kiss, swallowing her sounds of pleasure. It's not a gentle kiss. I'm branding her, possessing her, making her irrevocably mine.

I groan, feeling myself release inside her. It's like nothing I've ever felt before—raw and intense, consuming every part of me. We collapse together, but I keep my arms wrapped around her. She's still hugging me tightly, panting and sweaty, but neither of us moves. This moment is perfect, and I don't want it to end.

I pull back to look at her, our emotions clear in our eyes. I lean in to kiss her with the depth of our feelings. As our tongues dance together, I'm caught in a whirlwind of sensation—a heady blend of desire, intensity, and a deep, resonant love. Each emotion pours into the kiss, mingling, overwhelming, until I'm completely lost in the moment. When we finally part, gasping for air, I realize, with a shattering clarity, that by this act, I've become hers.

We've irrevocably given ourselves over to each other.

There's something undeniably thrilling about it too. The risk of letting someone in so deeply . . .

The realization sinks into my bones and deep in my soul as our afterglow finally crashes us. I break the kiss, pressing my forehead to hers, our panting breaths intermingling. No words are needed. What we've shared transcends anything that can be said.

"I love you," I say, knowing she'll brush it off, but hoping she won't run away.

Indie's smile is something completely different from

anything I've seen. When she speaks, her words cut through me, devastating and healing in the same breath. "I love you too," she says, and just like that, my soul feels both undone and rebuilt, intricately entwined with hers.

Chapter Forty-Five

Tyberius

I LACE UP MY SKATES, each pull of the laces tight and precise, like I'm preparing for battle. The cold air of the arena bites at my exposed skin, a familiar chill that's both a welcome and a warning. It's game day against the Boston Blizzards, and the tension is a thick fog in the locker room, palpable and heavy.

I'm out on the ice now, cutting through the silence

with the sharp scrape of my blades. The arena looms around me, the fans are ready for the game to start. Taking selfies of themselves against the players who are stretching, shooting toward the goalie and just making sure we're ready to face off the Boston Blizzards.

It's one of those Friday games when we're at home and Indie is able to visit since her parents offer to watch Myra. Even before I began to date their daughter, Jacob and Pria Decker took it upon themselves to give my child the family she's been wanting for so long. Now . . . they are hoping that soon we'll tell them things are more serious between us.

All that is up to Indie though. I'm doing this at her pace.

The buzzer sounds, and it's time to go back so the game can start. I glance toward the bench, right above it is Indie. Gloves and everything, I blow her a kiss and she does the same.

"Stay the fuck away from my sister," Jude mumbles as I walk by him.

I shake my head but say nothing. He's learning to deal with it.

WE'RE in the thick of it now. I'm on the offensive, my eyes scanning the ice for openings, for that split-second gap in the Blizzards' defense that I can exploit. My teammates are in sync, our time of playing together a silent language only we speak. A nod from Jenkins, a subtle shift from Rodney, and I know what to do.

I take the puck, feeling its weight and promise against my stick. The defense is closing in, a wall of jerseys and determination. I feint left, a move I've perfected over countless games, and then I'm through, breaking past their line with the puck still firmly under my control.

The goalie looms ahead, a final challenge to best. My heart pounds, a drumbeat of anticipation and adrenaline. I shoot. The puck flies, a blur of potential, and then—the unmistakable sound of the buzzer, the puck hitting the back of the net.

The crowd erupts, a wave of sound and fury, but all I hear is my team, their shouts and cheers grounding me. We circle together, to celebrate.

"This is it, boys," I say, my voice steady despite the pounding of my heart. "We keep this up, and we keep it home."

After the goal, the game's intensity doesn't just simmer; it boils, each minute ticking by ramping up the pressure. Frederick Rossi, one of the defensemen for the Boston Blizzards, has been a thorn in our side since the puck first dropped, his hits bordering on the excessive, his sneers . . . I've tried my best to brush him off and ignore him. More so when I want to kill him for what he did to Indie.

I have to keep my mind off my personal life, even when what he did should be punished—preferably by me. I focus on the game, but there's a line, and Rossi, with his latest cheap shot on Jenkins, has just crossed it.

I see red, but it's not just anger—it's a fierce protectiveness for my team, and my family. Before I fully grasp the decision, I'm skating toward him, my gloves hitting the ice with a thud that echoes my heartbeat. The crowd roars as a backdrop to the inevitable clash.

Rossi turns, a smirk playing on his lips, clearly

underestimating the situation. "Looking for trouble, Brynes?" His taunt is a spark to my already blazing fury.

"This isn't about trouble," I shoot back, closing the distance. "It's about respect." And with that, the gloves are off—quite literally. Our helmets clash.

We trade blows, his helmet comes off and I'm about to punch him when I hear a voice tell me, *Don't fuck this up.*

The referees are quick to intervene, their hands working to separate us. But even as they pull us apart, I still want to kill him.

Breathing hard, I glance over at Jenkins, who gives a nod of thanks. But as much as this was for him, it was more so for her. As I'm escorted to the penalty box, the crowd's mixture of boos and cheers washes over me, but I'm unfazed.

Sitting there, the adrenaline slowly recedes, giving way to a moment of clarity. The penalty minutes tick by, and I have a moment to gather my thoughts. I watch the game from the sidelines. When I come out, the coach and Jude call me to the bench.

"What the fuck was that?" Jude's voice is loud and angry.

My jaw ticks but I don't say anything.

"You were looking for blood. That's not what hockey is all about," he chides me.

"If you knew, you'd want to help me—and, yes, it was fucking personal."

His eyes narrow. I make the mistake of glancing over at where Indie sits next to Harper, who is holding her. Shit. I wasn't thinking.

"What does Rossi have to do with Indie and you?" Jude asks.

"Not my story to tell," I mumble. "Can I go back to play?"

He shakes his head. "Nope. You're benched for the rest of the game. I can't have you go to jail. I'm doing this for Myra and Indie, not for you."

Chapter Forty-Six

Indigo

THINGS I DIDN'T PLAN to do today: confess what happened with Frederick to my sisters—in the middle of a hockey game. Having to face my brother who is planning his ex-friend's demise. And of course, now my entire family knows exactly what happened when I was eighteen.

"I'm sorry," Ty says as we drive toward my house.

"I wish I could say that I don't understand your actions or that I'm angry about it, but . . ." My voice trails with uncertainty because I don't know how to finish that sentence. "I was just afraid you'd do something you'd regret and jeopardize your career because of me."

Does that make me a bad person? I enjoyed seeing the fear in Frederick's eyes when Ty had his jersey in one hand and was about to punch him hard in the face.

Ty grasps my hand, his calloused thumb caressing my knuckles in a tender gesture. "I would do anything for you, babe. But you're right, I shouldn't have lost control like that. Now I have to attend anger management classes and pay a fine to the team."

"The league fined you too?" I ask, brows furrowing. "Those fights happen often and it stopped before it got too out of hand."

"No, that was your brother's doing—to set an example," Ty grumbles, a muscle twitching along his stubbled jaw. "Though behind closed doors, he told me he appreciated me defending his little sister. However, he and the Quads are taking charge of the situation, whatever that means."

Gabe, Jude, our cousin Seth, and Piper are known as the Decker Quads. I honestly don't know what to expect, but probably a visit to Frederick to scare him shitless. Who knows with those four.

"I ruined today," Ty says remorsefully as we approach my house.

"You didn't," I assure him, squeezing his hand.

"I had plans for us. To take you up in a helicopter to Luna Harbor for a romantic overnight getaway—no worries, just the two of us. I wanted it to be perfect."

I sense his self-recrimination and gently ask, "Why can't we still do that?"

"Your brother mentioned they don't have enough staff to cover for me," he mutters. "I want to show you that I'm not a violent thug, but I understand why you'd think that after today."

And I think what happened earlier might've scared him more than me—or anyone in my family. I unbuckle my seat belt and slide onto his lap, cradling his rugged face in my hands. "Ty, I know you. How caring you are and how you would never hurt me—not even by accident."

I meet his uncertain gaze. "Was I frazzled after the fight?" I nod. "Of course, but mostly because you were too angry and I was afraid of what you could do to him. You're still Tyberius Brynes. The man who held my hand—virtually—while I finally faced my fears and found myself. You're an amazing father and the man I love with all my heart."

"I love you so fucking much, Indie," he rasps, the rawness in his voice squeezing my chest.

Unable to resist the magnetic pull between us, I press my lips to his in a tender, reassuring kiss.

"Would it be too soon to ask you to marry me, darling?" His green eyes search mine hopefully.

"Probably," I reply with an apologetic smile, affectionately stroking his scruffy jaw.

"How about moving in with us then?" He lifts my hand, brushing his lips over my knuckles in a featherlight caress that makes my pulse leap.

"I'd love that, as long as we can make that big house feel like ours," I propose, joy blossoming in my heart at the thought of our lives intertwining.

Ice, Love, & Other Penalties

WE SPEND Saturday and Sunday morning arranging the primary room and moving some of my stuff so I can move in with Ty. When we pick up Myra, I show her everything that we've done and she smiles. "Finally. Are you going to be my mom too?"

I glance at Ty, because we agreed that until he talks to her about their real relationship I'm not going to step into any role.

"She knows already. That's a surprise we had for you," he states. "We talked last week with Dr. Lindt about it, didn't we, pumpkin?"

"Yeah. He's like Uncle Gabe and Aunt Ameline to Cora, my best friend. I'm so special that instead of being his niece I'm his daughter—he chose me." Then she gives me a hopeful look. "Will you choose me?"

I open my arms and hug her. "As long as you choose me too, I will. Love you so much, Myra."

"Can I call you mom?"

"I'd be honored," I say, and I can't help but cry.

Ty joins us in the family hug and I'm not sure how this will look in the future, but right now I'm happy to have them, to be with them—hopefully forever.

Epilogue

Indigo

Two months later...

The alarm's harsh blare jolts me awake. I groan, burrowing deeper into Ty's warm embrace. His muscular arms tighten around me, pulling my back flush against his bare, sculpted chest.

"Just five more minutes," he mumbles, his voice a

Ice, Love, & Other Penalties

gravelly rasp from sleep that sends tingles skittering down my spine.

I can't help but smile, reveling in the feeling of his hard body pressed against my softer curves. His legs tangle lazily with mine under the sheets, not an inch of space left between us. I breathe him in—that masculine scent I love, sandalwood and spices with a hint of something uniquely Ty.

It's been two months since I moved in, and every day, I fall more and more in love with him. So many things have changed since I first stepped into this house. We stopped searching for a nanny. We share parental duties. However, those days when neither one of us can pick up Myra from school, my parents or siblings give us a hand.

Rolling over in his arms, I meet his sleepy green eyes, crinkled at the corners, as he flashes me that crooked grin that never fails to make my heart skip.

"Good morning, beautiful," he murmurs, his fingers reaching out to tenderly tuck back a lock of my hair. They linger, tracing the sensitive shell of my ear in a featherlight caress that has my pulse kicking up a notch.

"Mmm . . . Good morning." I lean in, brushing my lips against his. He responds immediately, capturing my mouth in a slow, deep kiss that steals my breath. My hands glide up his sculpted back, feeling the play of muscle under skin.

All too soon, he pulls back from the kiss with a regretful sigh, glancing ruefully at the clock.

"As much as I'd love to continue this, we need to get Myra ready for school," he says apologetically.

I pout playfully up at him through my lashes. "Does she really have to go today?"

He gives me a peck on the nose. "Yes, and according to your colorful and efficient chart, it's your turn to make breakfast."

I pull the blankets over my head with an exaggerated huff. "Not today, babe."

"Could I convince you to switch up the chores today . . . ? I have a really good incentive for you," I add, lowering my voice to a flirtatious purr as I peer up at him invitingly.

His grin turns wolfish, green eyes dancing. "Oh, really? And what did you have in mind as proper compensation?"

I bite my lip, trailing a suggestive hand down his chest. "I'm sure I could . . . come up with something."

He chuckles, the sound sending delicious vibrations through me. "Mmm, I bet you could, naughty girl." After another quick, toe-curling kiss, he throws off the covers and climbs out of bed. I admire the view as he saunters to the bathroom, all lean muscle and casual confidence.

Yeah, I'm definitely a fan of morning Ty.

"Is that a 'yes, Indie, I'll handle the morning chores and tonight you'll reward me?'" I pretend to sound like him but fail miserably.

He chuckles. "Nope. It's a, 'as much as I would love to take your offer, it's customary not to change our routine on game days,'" he responds.

"Since when did you become so superstitious, Brynes?" I ask slightly annoyed.

"When my lucky charm knocked on my door before our first game," he responds from the bathroom. "But . . . tonight I'll reward you after our win."

Ice, Love, & Other Penalties

I laugh. "Really, you think I'll be the one getting the reward?"

Ty pokes his head out of the bathroom, toothbrush in hand.

"Is that doubt I detect in your voice, Indie?" he asks, one brow arched. "Because I can assure you, after our win tonight, we'll both be thoroughly . . . 'rewarded.'"

His gaze turns molten, trailing hotly down my body in blatant invitation before meeting my eyes again. Even from across the room, that look sends heat curling through me.

I smirk, snuggling back under the blankets. "Promises, promises."

He winks. "Oh, I fully intend on keeping this one, sweetheart. In vivid detail."

With that heated promise lingering temptingly in the air between us, he disappears back into the bathroom. I hear the shower turn on a moment later.

As I lay there listening to him start his morning routine, I can't stop the little thrill that goes through me at the thought of properly "celebrating" with Ty tonight. Game days when he's at home have become my favorite. And if our team wins . . . Well, neither of us are getting much sleep.

Ty insists that the day I appeared at his doorstep I changed his life, but it was mutual. My life has slowly shifted. I'm back to taking classes. Lyr, Harp, and I are planning on starting our company. And even though I adore Jude and would do anything for him, I already gave him my . . . Well, it's not exactly a two-week notice. Once the Sasquatches finish their season—hopefully after winning the Stanley Cup—I'm no longer working for him. We're already looking for my replacement.

Tyberius

The moonlight shimmers off the gentle waves, illuminating Indie's face in an ethereal glow as we stroll along the beach, the sand soft beneath our bare feet. This is a small break before the finals start next week. We still don't know who'll be playing, but before I have to head back home and concentrate on our last seven games, I wanted to steal this quiet moment with Indie.

I stop and take her hands in mine, chills skittering up my spine. Our eyes meet and the nerves dissolve, warmth rushing in to take their place.

"From the first moment I saw you, I knew," I begin, pulse quickening, every word layered with the love and adoration I have for her.

Indie tilts her head, a smile playing at her lips. "Knew what?" Curiosity and something deeper shine in her eyes.

A smile finds its way to my lips, and I reach up to brush a windblown curl from her cheek, tucking it behind her ear gently. "That you were the one to complete our puzzle. Just like when you found the right piece for Myra. You . . . you were my missing piece," I confess, the words flowing from a place deep within my heart. "I've never felt so whole. In your eyes, I've found my home. In your smile, I've found my peace. And in your love, I've found the very essence of my being."

I drop to one knee, nerves and elation warring

within me, and from my pocket, I retrieve a small box. Nestled inside is a delicate princess-cut diamond solitaire on a simple platinum band, an understated elegance befitting my Indie.

"Indie, you are my dawn, my sunset, and every moment in between. With you, I've discovered parts of me I never knew existed. Your love has been my guiding light, illuminating the darkest paths, leading me to this very moment."

I meet her shimmering gaze. "Will you do me the honor, the privilege, of becoming my partner, my confidante, my best friend, a mother to our children, for life?" My voice cracks with emotion. "I offer to you not just a ring, but my heart, my soul, and every beat of my being."

Indie's eyes, wide with emotion, glisten in the moonlight, reflecting a universe of feelings that words could scarcely contain. Tears begin their descent, tracing paths down her cheeks. For a heartbeat, the world stands still, suspended as I wait anxiously for her answer.

"Yes, Ty," she whispers. "Yes, I will marry you."

She launches herself into my arms. I stand and catch her effortlessly, my hands finding her waist as her legs wrap around me. We twirl in joyful circles, laughter bubbling over. When we finally still, her palms come up to cradle my jaw. Our smiles melt away as her lips meet mine in a kiss that steals the breath from my lungs.

My hand splays across the small of her back, pressing her closer as my other hand tangles in her windswept hair. Our kiss deepens, all the longing and passion that has built between us finally finding release.

It's like our first kiss, uncertain yet exhilarating. It's

like our last kiss, desperate and full of goodbye. But also like no other kiss, full of promise—the promise of a future together.

The promise of forever, of us.

When we break apart, her eyes shine like stars and I know she's happy.

"I love you, so much," I whisper, resting my forehead against hers.

She smiles, brushing her nose against mine. "I love you too—for always."

I return her smile. While gazing deeply into her eyes, I'm reminded as to why I'm so thankful, thinking back on how we got to where we are.

Where we, eventually, allowed the ice to thaw around our previous beliefs about romantic love.

Where we, finally, found the love we both denied ourselves and opened up our hearts to one another.

Claudia is an award-winning, *USA Today* bestselling author.

She writes alluring, thrilling stories about complicated women and the men who take their breaths away. Her books are the perfect blend of steamy and heartfelt, filled with emotional characters and explosive chemistry. Her writing takes readers to new heights, providing a variety of tears, laughs, and shocking moments that leave fans on the edge of their seats.

She lives in Denver, Colorado with her husband, her youngest two children, and three fluffy dogs.

When Claudia is not writing, you can find her reading, knitting, or just hanging out with her family. At nights, she likes to binge watches shows or movies with her equally geeky husband.

To find more about Claudia:
    website

Be sure to sign up for my newsletter where you'll receive news about upcoming releases, sneak previous, and also FREE books from other bestselling authors.

Also By Claudia Burgoa

Be sure to sign up for my newsletter where you'll receive news about upcoming releases, sneak previous, and also FREE books from other bestselling authors.

Ice, Love, & Other Penalties is also available in Audio

The Baker's Creek Billionaire Brothers Series

Loved You Once

A Moment Like You

Defying Our Forever

Call You Mine

As We Are

Yours to Keep

Collide with Me

Paradise Bay Billionaire Brothers

My Favorite Night

Faking The Game

Can't Help Love

Along Came You

My Favorite Mistake

The Way of Us

Meant For Me

Finally Found You

Where We Belong

Heartwood Lake Secret Billionaires

A Place Like You

Dirty Secret Love

Love Unlike Ours

Through It All

Better than Revenge

Fade into us

An Unlikely Story

Hard to love

Against All Odds Series

Wrong Text, Right Love

Didn't Expect You

Love Like Her

Until Next Time, Love

Something Like Love

Accidentally in Love

Decker Family Novels

Unexpected Everlasting:

Suddenly Broken

Suddenly Us

Somehow Everlasting:
Almost Strangers
Strangers in Love

Perfect Everlasting:
Who We Are
Who We Love

Us After You

Covert Affair Duet:
After The Vows
Love After Us

The Downfall of Us:
The End of Me
When Forever Finds Us

Requiem for Love:
Reminders of Her
The Symphony of Us

Impossibly Possible:
The Lies About Forever
The Truth About Love

Ice, Love, & Other Penalties

Second Chance Sinners :
Pieces of Us
Somehow Finding Us

The Spearman Brothers

Maybe Later
Then He Happened
Once Upon a Holiday
Almost Perfect

Luna Harbor

Finally You
Perfectly You
Always You
Truly You

My One
My One Regret
My One Desire

The Everhart Brothers

Fall for Me
Fight for Me

Perfect for Me

Forever with Me

Kentbury Tales

Christmas in Kentbury

Fall in Kentbury

Standalones

Chasing Fireflies

Until I Fall

Finding My Reason

Something Like Hate

Someday, Somehow

Chaotic Love Duet

Begin with You

Back to You

Co-writing

Holiday with You

Home with You

Here with You

All my books are interconnected standalone, except for the duets, but if you want a reading order, I have it here ↪
Reading Order

Printed in Great Britain
by Amazon